This is my book
Debbie W.
Y0-BDI-273

The Horse on the Roof

The Horse on the Roof

BOB WELLS

Illustrated by
Bernice Loewenstein

J. B. LIPPINCOTT COMPANY
Philadelphia & New York

PRINTED IN THE UNITED STATES OF AMERICA
Library of Congress Catalog Card Number 78–117243
First Edition

To Nancy
and her horses

The Horse on the Roof

one

Great-Uncle Buck Denton walked through the door of the new apartment. He glared around. He waggled his beard. He ran his hand impatiently through his bushy white hair.

"This Manhattan place doesn't look one bit like the Denton house back home," he declared. "I'll have to make some changes."

Sylvester Denton came into Apartment 12-B next. He was a little out of breath from walking up twelve flights of stairs to the top floor of Whetstone Manor. He'd had to walk because his favorite bamboo fishing pole wouldn't fit in the elevator.

Sylvester's wife, Charlene, hurried into the apartment a few steps behind him. She began inspecting the rooms. The light wasn't going to be good for her geraniums, she told her son, Harvey, who followed her around, carrying a large wooden box.

"Where am I going to put my frogs, Ma?" he demanded.

Melinda, who was two years, six weeks, and fourteen days older than Harvey, arrived last. She was a pretty girl, with dark hair and a thoughtful expression. Like the others, she decided the apartment wasn't really what she'd had in mind. But there was no use complaining.

She walked into the back bedroom, carrying her two suitcases. Out of one of them she took twelve books about horses and fourteen framed pictures of horses. She put the books on a shelf and fastened the pictures to the wall. Then she went to the other suitcase and removed forty-seven plaster models of horses, which she arranged as best she could. Now the room looked a lot more homelike, she decided. The apartment wasn't much like the house in Baffles Falls, but it wasn't completely hopeless after all.

The movers brought the furniture. Mrs. Denton fixed supper. After the dishes were washed, the family sat around the living room discussing the situation.

"The fishing isn't going to be as good as I'd hoped," Sylvester said. "Do you suppose we could run a fish line from the front window, across the park, over the highway, and down to the Hudson River so I could fish from the living room? What do you think, Uncle Buck?"

"I think this place hasn't got a place to pitch my hammock," Buck Denton said. "And furthermore—"

"And furthermore," Harvey said, "my frogs aren't used to living on the twelfth floor."

"I wonder whether anybody'd mind if I nailed some window boxes to the outside," Mrs. Denton said. "What do you think, Melinda?"

"I think I'm a long way from getting the horse I've always wanted. I didn't have a horse back home and I don't see how I'm ever going to get one now we're living in New York City."

"Always talking about horses," Harvey said. "Can a horse catch flies with its tongue? Can a horse hold its breath and swim underwater?"

"Well, can a frog gallop around a pasture? Can a frog eat oats or nuzzle up to you?"

"It could nuzzle if it had a mind to, only it doesn't go for sissy stuff like that."

"A horse is better than a frog," Melinda said. "And some day I'm going to have one."

It was a fine conversation the Dentons had and it lasted until bedtime because no one got bored with the talk. Each one spoke of whatever interested him. Sylvester considered fishing more important than gardening and his wife considered flowers and plants more important than recollections of how things had been in Baffles Falls. Great-Uncle Buck considered discussions of small town life more interesting than talk about petunias or snap-dragons and Harvey felt that frogs were more important than anything. As for Melinda, she didn't care what they talked about, as long as it had to do with horses.

Before many days had gone by, Apartment 12-B looked different. There were geraniums and begonias on each windowsill. There was an ivy plant that began in a pot in the living room, wound through the kitchen and dining room, looped over the door and behind the horse pictures in Melinda's room and wound up triumphantly in the shower, where the humidity suited it just fine.

On one wall of the living room were three stuffed fish. In a makeshift swamp under Harvey's bed was a flourishing colony of frogs, who sang pleasantly all night. Melinda had her horse pictures and horse books and that left only Uncle Buck at loose ends. He still hadn't been able to figure out a way to make New York City seem like his boyhood home in the country.

"I don't care what you say," he told Melinda. "New York just isn't much like Baffles Falls."

"There wouldn't be very good pasture here for my horse, if I had a horse."

"A man wasn't meant to stay cooped up inside four walls. He ought to be able to take a stroll on his own land. He ought to have a front porch to sit on. He ought to have a hammock so he can lie back and think about things until he goes to sleep."

"He ought to have a horse, too."

"You're doggoned right he ought to," Great-Uncle Buckmaster told her, waggling his beard. "And just maybe—I'm not promising nothing, mind you—just maybe you and me are going to have one."

Up to this point, Melinda hadn't paid much attention to the conversation, which had been a lot like so many other conversations. Now she jumped up from the sofa and stood in front of Buck Denton.

"Really?" Her voice sounded louder and shriller than she'd intended. "You really mean it?"

"Don't go getting all in a lather, girl. I just said maybe. And it might be just as well if you kept your voice down on account of your dad and ma don't know a thing about it."

"But how are you going to get us a horse, Uncle Buck? Horses cost money and besides—"

"Never you mind. All I can say is, I've taken steps. It won't do you no good to ask questions because the time's not ripe just yet for the deal to come through. Now, to get back to what I was saying, a man ought to have a little land around him to live the way a man ought to live."

"I think so, too. Especially if he has a horse to raise."

"I told you to forget about horses." Buck seemed a little uneasy about the topic. "Let's talk about getting ourselves a little place in the country—that's the first thing to worry about."

"But how can we do that? Dad signed a two-year lease for this apartment. Besides, he has his job here and everything."

"Oh, we've got to stay in the city, no two ways about that. But the question is, can we find ourselves a place in the country without leaving the city?"

Melinda said she didn't see how anyone could be in two places at once—although if someone was riding a fast horse, he could be in one place one minute and another place the next. But Uncle Buck ignored the opportunity to talk about horses.

"In my day, I've seen a lot of places and done a lot of things," he said. "I've seen things happen that once looked impossible. When I was a boy, if somebody'd told me they'd send voices and pictures through the air without anything but a TV tower at one end and some kid fiddling with a dial at the other, I'd've said they was talking foolishness. So the point I'm making is that maybe we can have us a little bit of the country even in New York if only we can find some vacant space nobody's using."

"It seems like everybody's using just about all the space there is around here," Melinda said.

"Maybe so and maybe not. How high up have you been in this building?"

"We're already on the top floor, Uncle Buck."

"Yes, but what's above the top floor?"

"The roof, I suppose."

"And what's on the roof?"

"I don't know."

Great-Uncle Buckmaster glanced around, ran his hand through his bushy white hair, waggled his beard back and forth, then leaned toward her. He lowered his voice to a whisper.

"Let's you and me go up there and find out," he said.

two

There wasn't much of anything worth looking at on the flat roof of Whetstone Manor. In one corner were some rusty poles and sagging wires that had once been used for hanging wet clothes on wash day, but no one had used them since the management had installed electric dryers in the basement. There were several rusty tin cans. There was a stone parapet going all the way around the roof, high enough so it would be necessary to go to some trouble to fall off. There was a chimney over in one corner. There was quite a lot of dust and soot. But mostly the roof was empty.

Great-Uncle Buckmaster climbed out of the wide trapdoor and looked around. Melinda stood beside him, her face showing disappointment.

"It doesn't look like much," she said.

"No, it doesn't, girl. You're right about that. But you got to give it one thing in its favor—it's vacant."

"You were talking about vacant land. This is just dirty roofing paper."

"Right again. But let's not give up too easy. What would it take to make this empty space here into a piece of countryside?"

"A miracle, I guess."

"That'd sure be nice. But I had in mind something involving a little hard work and elbow grease, which are the kind of things I'm more used to. Now what's the first thing a country fellow does when he decides to start a homestead?"

"Picks out a good piece of farmland?"

"If he can find one. And if he can't, he makes do with what he can get. Then the thing he does after he gets his site picked out is see what kind of a deal he can work out with whoever owns it. I don't see any way clear to buy this roof, but maybe I could manage to rent it."

"I don't think anybody rents out roofs."

"You never know until you ask, girl."

"And even if Mr. Canelli, the landlord, would rent it to you, what would you do with it?"

"I've got something in mind. But I'll need some help, I expect." Great-Uncle Buckmaster peered at her slyly from the corners of his eyes. "What I need is a pretty young lady who ain't afraid of getting her hands dirty. I need the kind of helper in this rooftop wilderness that them pioneer fellows had, back when they were moving west."

Melinda said she'd be glad to do what she could, only she wished this was a real wilderness and he was a real pioneer so she could help him by riding across the prairie on a horse.

"You want to do what?" Mr. Canelli, the landlord, said when they went to see him. "I'm in the business of rentings things. I rent out three-room efficiencies, one-room studios, five-room apartments. But roofs? I never rented out a roof in my life."

"Then it'll be a new experience for both of us,"

Buck said. He took his hat from his left knee and balanced it on his right knee. "I never had to rent a roof before to get a little privacy and peace and open space."

"That's what we're all looking for, without expecting to find it." Mr. Canelli peered at his two visitors suspiciously. "You don't plan to do something to my roof that'll cause me trouble?"

"We won't hurt your roof, Mr. Canelli," Melinda said. "It's just that my great-uncle has to live in the city when he'd rather live in the country and he's trying to make the best of things."

"That's what we all do," the landlord said, leaning back in his swivel chair in his office. "We all try to make the best of things. If I could get a little rent money for a roof, I suppose that'd be all to the good—providing you didn't do anything that might cause me trouble. What did you have in mind as a fair rent for the property?"

"Eighteen dollars and sixty-five cents a month," Buck Denton said, promptly. "No more and no less."

"Any special reason for that figure?" Mr. Canelli asked.

"For one reason, I think that's a fair price. For another, a man shouldn't pay out more than a fourth of his income in rent. And eighteen dollars and sixty-five cents is exactly one-fourth of my pension check."

Mr. Canelli looked at Uncle Buck for quite a while without saying anything. Then he began to laugh.

"There's something about you I like," he said. "You talk straight from the shoulder like an honest man. I been in the business a long time, but I don't know a thing about renting out roofs. If you say a roof is worth eighteen dollars and sixty-five cents a month, then that's what it's worth. As long as it hasn't been bringing in a dime up to now, I guess I can't lose."

"You did what?" Sylvester said when he heard about the deal. "Why in the world do you want a roof, Uncle Buck? You can't go fishing up there."

"I suppose there's lots of sun to raise plants, though," Mrs. Denton said. "You wouldn't mind if I used a corner of it, I don't suppose."

"Frogs don't like too much sun," Harvey said. "Of course I might rig up a pool on the roof with an umbrella over it."

"All in good time," Buck said. "We ain't ready to start homesteading just yet. All we got right now is some vacant space."

"That's right," Melinda said. "We haven't even got a—"

But then she remembered her great-uncle had said not to tell anyone about the horse just yet. She let the sentence dangle, unfinished.

three

The first thing Great-Uncle Buckmaster did with his roof was string a hammock between two of the rusty metal clothes poles, lie back in it, and close his eyes. Melinda came through the trapdoor to see what he was up to. She tiptoed across the roof to where he was, so she wouldn't wake him if he was asleep. He opened one eye and looked at her, then closed it again.

"Sit down, girl. Make yourself comfortable. I'm lying here, thinking."

"I thought you were sleeping."

"Nothing of the sort. A man does his best thinking lying in a hammock, letting the breeze sway him just a little, looking up at the trees. Only there's no trees here, so I been doing the next best thing—I've been lying here with my eyes closed, seeing the trees in my mind's eye. The mind's eye is a wonderful thing, girl."

"I guess so."

"You know so. Try it." He hopped nimbly out of the hammock. "Lie down here, close your eyes and try it."

Melinda stretched out in the hammock. Her great-uncle asked her what she saw.

"Gray sky. A piece of rusty clothes pole."

"That's because you're looking at things with your open eye, not your mind's eye. Tune in your mind's eye, girl. It's better than the late, late show on television. Now tell me, what do you see?"

"A colt."

"I thought you might see something like that. What color is he?"

"Palomino. He's a beautiful palomino. The sun shines on his mane and tail and makes it look like silky gold."

"He's galloping, I guess."

"No, he isn't. He's just walking around, looking proud, next to some white fences and—" She opened her eyes. "Oh, I wish I had him, Uncle Buck. I know I never will, but it would be so wonderful."

Buckmaster Denton waggled his beard, glaring down at her fiercely.

"Somehow, some way, you're going to have a horse, girl. But first things first. Before we're ready for a horse, we've got to have a pasture."

Melinda sat up on the edge of the swaying hammock.

"Then I guess it's hopeless. There isn't any pasture around here."

"Not now, there ain't. So what we've got to do is build us one."

"I don't see how we can do that."

"First off, what do you need to have a pasture?"

"A piece of land, I suppose."

"Right. And how deep does the piece of land have to be?"

"You mean how big?"

"Nope. I mean how deep."

"All the way down to China, I guess."

"Wrong. If it was a foot deep, that'd be plenty. Eight

or ten inches'd be enough. Even six might do it, grass being a shallow-rooted kind of weed."

"I never heard of a pasture only six or eight inches deep, Uncle Buck."

"That's because you haven't spent enough time lying in a hammock, looking at your mind's eye. You study the matter and you realize that all a pasture is, when you come right down to it, is a few inches of topsoil, with something to hold the topsoil up. What usually holds it up is some more dirt and pebbles and rocks and on down to the center of the earth. But the grass don't care what's holding it up, so long as the topsoil's there. The grass wouldn't know the difference if that few inches of topsoil was twelve stories up in the air, being held up by a roof that some old codger had rented for eighteen dollars and sixty-five cents a month."

Melinda jumped out of the hammock. She put her arms around her great-uncle's shoulders.

"Why, that's wonderful. That's the most wonderful thing I've ever heard."

"Hold your horses, girl. All I been saying is true. I saw it all in my mind's eye, lying there in the hammock. I saw eight or ten inches of topsoil spread over this whole roof. I saw somebody planting grass seed in that topsoil—a fellow with a beard was doing the seeding and a pretty young girl was helping him. I saw that seed sprout and grow tall. But there was one thing I couldn't see in my mind's eye, lying there in the hammock."

"What was that, Uncle Buck?"

"I couldn't see how in the world you and me was going to get us enough dirt to spread around this roof and make a pasture."

Melinda sank back down on the hammock. She looked

across the expanse of dingy roofing paper. She had never in her life seen anything that looked less like a pasture.

"Then I guess we can't do it," she said.

"Who said we can't? Just because we aren't smart enough to think of a way doesn't mean there isn't one. What we need is a little help from some expert who knows more about dirt than we do."

"Ma know about planting things in it."

"She surely does. But this ain't the kind of thing a mother can help with much. Mothers know about planting things in dirt. They know about getting rid of dirt. But they don't know how you go about getting dirt in the first place."

"I guess Dad wouldn't be the one to ask, either."

"Nope. My nephew'd be the one to tell you where to find a grassy bank to sit down on and dangle a line in a brook. But he's not the one to help us with this problem we got right now."

"The Department of Agriculture, then? We could write a letter to Washington."

"They aren't the ones, either. They got a lot of scientists and people who know how to raise more corn and wheat and soybeans in dirt. But they don't pay much mind to the problem of how you go about getting some dirt in the first place."

"There isn't anybody else to ask, I guess. It looks to me like we're out of luck."

"That's where you're wrong, girl. Do you know who the greatest expert on the subject of dirt in the entire world is? A kid brother."

"Harvey? All he knows about is frogs."

"He's a boy, isn't he? It's been my experience that if there's any dirt lying around loose a boy will find it. It's instinct, like a monarch butterfly seekin' out a milkweed plant to lay her eggs."

Melinda wasn't convinced that her brother would be any help to them, but she followed Uncle Buck down through the trapdoor to the hall stairway and into Apartment 12-B. Harvey was busy trying to catch a housefly to feed to his frogs, but when they presented the problem to him he gave it some thought. Then he shook his head.

"I can't think of any place around here where you could get some dirt, Uncle Buck. There's plenty of dirt in the park, but I don't think they'd want you to dig it up and haul it up on your roof."

"What I had in mind was a big pile of dirt that nobody wanted."

"I don't know of any like that. I could ask around."

"You do that, boy. Meanwhile, I got a big favor to ask. It's going to require some sacrifice on your part, but I want you to do it without asking me any questions. Okay?"

"I guess so, if it's important."

"It's important, all right. Now here's what I want you to do."

Harvey turned pale when he heard what Buckmaster Denton had in mind. But he was a brave boy and he'd given his word. When he'd made his preparations and left the apartment, his great-uncle motioned to Melinda. They ran down the twelve flights of stairs and out on the sidewalk just in time to see Harvey turning the corner.

"We mustn't lose him, girl," Buck said. "I'm a little winded. You trot on ahead and keep him in sight—but don't let him know we're following."

When Melinda turned the corner, staying close to the buildings to be as inconspicuous as possible, she saw that she needn't have hurried. Harvey was dawdling along, looking in store windows. He stopped for several minutes to watch a pigeon that was strutting back and forth across a ledge on a building. He picked up a candy wrapper that had blown into the gutter and read every word that was printed on it. He moved on down the sidewalk aimlessly. Uncle Buck had caught up to Melinda by then. They followed Harvey at a safe distance.

"I don't see how this is going to help us," Melinda said, rather impatiently. "He doesn't act like he knows where he's going. He's just fooling around."

"You've got to trust nature, girl. When you've spent part of your life farming, like I have, you begin to understand that there are certain natural laws and if you can figure out what they are and go along with them, you get along just fine."

"I don't think natural laws have much to do with kid brothers," Melinda said.

Harvey was still stopping now and then to look at things, but he was moving a little faster now. He still didn't seem to have any destination in mind, but he was walking more purposefully. Melinda and Uncle Buck increased their pace to keep up with him, but they had to keep from being seen so they couldn't follow too closely. It was perhaps twenty minutes after Harvey had left the apartment house when he turned a corner and disappeared. When Melinda got there she couldn't see him anywhere.

"Now where did he go? He isn't on the sidewalk up ahead of us."

"We mustn't lose him," Uncle Buck said. "Come on, let's run."

Several passersby turned to look in curiosity at the girl

and the bearded man trotting along, peering anxiously in all directions. Melinda glanced up at her great-uncle. He didn't seem to mind in the least that people were looking at him.

"We've lost him," Melinda said, slowing down. "He just isn't any place."

Uncle Buck stopped short.

"Oh, no? Then who's that kid over there, standing on top of as fine a pile of topsoil as I've seen since we left Baffles Falls?"

Melinda started toward her brother. Then she stopped and looked at her great-uncle in wonderment.

"You knew all the time he'd find it. How could you possibly know he'd come right straight here?"

"The laws of nature, girl. All you got to do is go along with the laws of nature."

"But Harvey said he didn't know where there was any dirt."

"Of course he didn't. But nature knew. You don't fool old Mother Nature about a thing like that."

"But if Harvey didn't know where that dirt pile was, how—?"

"Very simple. You remember what I made him do, back at the apartment? I made him take a bath, even though that's a lot to ask of a boy, especially in the middle of the afternoon. And then you recollect I had him put on his very best clothes—white shirt, clean pants, even a necktie. And then you remember what I said?"

"You said he was to be very careful to stay absolutely clean until suppertime."

"Right. And that's where the laws of nature took over. The laws of boy's nature, to be exact. Any boy Harvey's age who's just taken a bath and put on his best clothes and been told under no circumstances to get dirty has just got to follow his instinct. He hasn't got the slightest choice about it."

"And his instinct is to head for the nearest dirt pile, whether he knows it's there or not?"

"Right," Uncle Buck said, waggling his beard at her. "And so now we've got ourselves a source of supply for making us a pasture and all we've got to do is figure out a way to get it from here to our roof."

four

Melinda and her great-uncle went back to the dirt pile early the next morning. A crew of workmen were busily excavating a hole. Machines were snarling. Men were hurrying around. No one paid the slightest attention to the bearded man and the girl.

"Who are we going to ask?" Melinda inquired. "Everybody looks so busy."

"We're going to ask the guy in charge," Uncle Buck said. "He'll be the one who's not doing any work. It's been my experience that if you pick out the fellow who looks like he's loafing you'll find out he's the boss."

"Then it must be that fellow over there." Melinda pointed to a tall man with a sunburned face. "He's just standing around, watching the bulldozer driver and the crane operator and the rest of them."

Buck walked quickly over to where the man was standing.

"You the boss of this here lash-up?"

Rusty O'Malley took off his hard hat and wiped his forehead with a bandanna handkerchief.

"I'm the contractor who's building an apartment house here. What can I do for you?"

"I'm in the market for some dirt. It appears to me like you got a pretty good pile of it."

"I sure have. I'm planning on hauling it over to Jersey and dumping it."

"That must be a nuisance, having to tote it clear over there," Buck said. "I could show you a place to dump it only six blocks from here."

"Friend, if you can show me a dump site that close, I'll haul all the dirt you can use there and I won't charge you a cent."

"It's only fair to warn you, the place I got in mind is a mite hard to get at."

"So's Jersey, what with all the traffic my trucks have got to contend with. Let's take a look at this vacant lot you've got that can use some fill."

O'Malley drove Melinda and Buck back to their apartment house. He parked his car on the crowded street, climbed out, and looked around.

"I know this neighborhood pretty well," he said, "but I never knew there was any open space around here. You sure you've got a place for my dirt pile?"

"We sure have," Buck told him. "Come on inside and I'll show you."

"Inside?"

"We have to take the elevator," Melinda explained.

O'Malley stared at her and shook his head. But he followed them as they led the way into Whetstone Manor. When they climbed out of the trapdoor onto the roof he walked over to the edge and peered down.

"What is this, anyhow? I still don't see any vacant lot."

"That's because you're looking in the wrong place," Buck said. "You're standing right on the edge of as fine a piece of pasture land as there is between the Bronx and the Battery. All it needs is some grass seed and that dirt pile."

O'Malley's face got redder. He stalked over to Melinda and Buck. He glared down at them.

"I guess it takes all kinds of oddballs to make a world. But I sure don't see where it's funny for you to waste my time this way. I'm a busy man. I've got an apartment house to build."

"And I've got a pasture to build." Buck waggled his beard in the contractor's face. "I admit the notion of putting a pasture on top of a roof takes a little getting used to. But you got to agree this rooftop is a lot closer than New Jersey."

"You expect me to have my trucks fly up here and dump the dirt?"

"You might haul it with a helicopter," Melinda suggested.

"I don't have a helicopter. Up until now, I never saw a need for one in my business."

"You could dump the dirt on the sidewalk outside the apartment house. Then we could carry it up in the elevator, a bushel basket at a time."

Rusty O'Malley frowned down at her.

"Of all the silly ideas I ever heard, that's the silliest. It'd take you twenty years to haul that dirt pile up here in bushel baskets. Besides, who ever heard of dumping dirt on a roof?"

"Like I say, it does take some getting used to," Buck admitted. "It takes a man with a little imagination to picture it. If you was to lie down in that hammock over there, it might be easier."

"I haven't got time to lie around in a hammock."

"That's too bad," Melinda said. "Uncle Buck gets some

of his best ideas there. That's how he figured out how we could have a country place in the city."

"You remind me of Mary, my daughter," O'Malley told her. "You're about the same age. You talk a lot alike. As long as I've gone this far, I suppose you might as well go ahead and tell me what you've got in mind. Not that I expect it to make much sense."

"I've always wanted a horse," Melinda began.

"Now you really do sound like Mary. Every girl your age thinks she's got to have a horse, no matter how impractical it is. Don't tell me you expect to keep one up here?"

"We could if we had a pasture. And we could have a pasture on this rooftop if it was covered with a few inches of dirt. The grass wouldn't care that it was twelve stories up in the air."

"I guess I will lie down in that hammock," O'Malley said. "The more I hear of this scheme, the harder it is to believe."

He walked over to the hammock and stretched out in it. The sun was in his eyes, so he closed them.

"Just for the sake of argument, suppose you had this roof covered with dirt. What would you do then?"

"We'd build a white board fence, I guess," Melinda said. "And some kind of a stable. And we'd plant the grass seed."

"This rooftop belongs to you?"

"We've rented it," Buck said.

O'Malley closed his eyes, after opening them to look at Buck and Melinda. "I should never have stretched out in this hammock. When I lie here with my eyes shut I can see this roof growing hay, and that's crazy. I ought to have my head examined for even listening to such nonsense."

"I'll bet your daughter would like to come over here

and see it when it's finished," Melinda said. "I'll bet she'd like to help groom my horse. When I get one, that is."

"I admit I don't know how we'd get the dirt pile from the street up here," Uncle Buck said. "I guess what we need is some smart engineer fellow who knows about such things."

"I know all there is to know about moving dirt around, friend." O'Malley swung his long legs over the side of the hammock and sat up. "I know about moving things and building things. What you'd need is a motor up here, with a cable fastened to a sling. The cable would be hooked up to a drum. The drum would turn around, winding up the cable and pulling the sling full of dirt up to the roof. It could be done."

"That'd be mighty expensive, I guess, rigging up a contraption like that," Buck said.

"It's mighty expensive having to haul that dirt all the way to Jersey. I don't know as it'd cost me much more to dump it here—maybe not as much."

Melinda's eyes were shining.

"Why, that's wonderful, Mr. O'Malley."

"Now don't go jumping to conclusions. I haven't said I'd do it. All I said was that it's possible. It still doesn't make any sense, making a pasture twelve stories up."

"Then the thing to do is lie back down there in that hammock," Uncle Buck said. "Just make yourself nice and comfortable. That's the way. Now close your eyes."

"I haven't got time for all this foolishness."

"You got as much time as anybody else has. Now take a good look at that pasture in your mind's eye. Take a look at the green shoots coming up in that dirt. It's city dirt, but the grass don't care. The seed starts a-sprouting and growing and first thing you know you're lying here with the breeze rocking you and you look off across this fine piece of pasture land and you're not in New York City any more. You're up on a hill in the country."

"A hill twelve stories high." O'Malley opened his eyes. "I'll say this for you, old-timer. You've come up with something new. If I helped you with this crazy project, I could at least say I'd helped build something nobody else around here has built. And that's my business, building things."

"Now you're talking," Buck said. "The minute I saw you loafing around over there near the dirt pile, watching everybody else work, I figured you were a man who'd know how to do things."

O'Malley laughed. He stood up. He walked over toward the trapdoor.

"You win. I guess Jersey doesn't need my dirt pile as much as you do. I'll put it up here, on one condition."

"Whatever it is," Melinda said, "we'll do it."

"All I'm asking is this: If you ever get that pasture built, which I doubt, Mary and I have the right to come up here and sit and watch the grass grow. Okay?"

"You can do better than that," Uncle Buck said, taking O'Malley's hand and shaking it. "When we get our grass plot established, you can come up here and take off your shoes and walk through it barefoot, if you've a mind to."

five

In Apartment 4-A, Kermit Hofreitz was reading the morning *Times* when he caught sight of something moving outside his living-room window. He jumped up and ran over to look. Then he shouted for his wife.

"Hey, there's a wire cable hanging down from the roof. What's going on here?"

Mrs. Hofreitz came in, wiping her hands on her apron.

"It's that Sylvester Denton, up on the top floor, I suppose," she said. "His wife was telling me he's been trying to figure out a way to get a fishing line from his apartment to the river."

Hofreitz took another look at the steel cable dangling past his window.

"He must be expecting to catch a whopper. With a fish line like that, he could haul in a whale."

"I wouldn't put it past him," Mrs. Hofreitz said, and went back to the kitchen to finish fixing breakfast.

In Apartment 8-B, Mrs. Selma Shapiro saw the first slingful of topsoil being hauled up past her window. Her daughter, Marcia, ran to look.

"What is it, Mother? It looks like hundreds of pounds of dirt. Who lives above us who'd want all that dirt?"

"I suppose it's Mrs. Denton. I knew she was crazy about growing house plants, but I didn't expect her to start a whole greenhouse full of geraniums up there."

"Should I run up and ask her?"

"Certainly not, Marcia. One of the rules of living in New York City is that you don't mind other people's business. If she wants all that dirt, let her have it. That's her affair."

"Mrs. Pontey, down on the sixth floor, is always minding other people's business."

"She isn't a real New Yorker. If she was, she'd know the only way you can live all crowded together on this island like we do is to let other people go their own way, as long as they let you go yours."

"Just the same," Marcia said, "I'd like to see all those flowers Mrs. Denton must be raising up there. I think I'll go up and visit Melinda."

In Apartment 6-B, Mrs. Joyce Pontey pushed open the window and watched the load of dirt rising on its steel cable. She leaned out and craned her neck to see where it was going. Then she looked down to where another dump truck filled with dirt had pulled up, ready to deliver the next load. She drew her head in and turned to her husband.

"Lester, you won't believe this, but somebody's dumping dirt on our roof."

"So?"

"I don't think it's right. If you won't do something about it, I will."

Lester Pontey sighed. He had learned that there was no use arguing when his wife made up her mind to mix into something that didn't concern her.

"You can do what you want to," he said. "But kindly leave me out of it."

"I've got a mind to call up Canelli, the landlord. There's nothing in our lease that says we're supposed to have to put up with this."

"You don't suppose anybody'd dump dirt on the roof of his building without Canelli authorizing it, do you? He's probably having a rooftop garden built up there. Some of those fancy apartments on the East Side have rooftop gardens, with trees growing and everything."

"But this isn't that kind of an apartment house."

"So call up Canelli and make a fool of yourself. Just keep my name out of it, that's all."

Mrs. Pontey stood there, pondering the matter. What was bothering her, she admitted to herself, was that she couldn't understand what was going on. She prided herself on knowing everybody's business at Whetstone Manor, but for once she'd been caught by surprise. As she watched, the empty sling descended on its cable to the ground, where it was refilled and started creaking skyward again.

"Oh, well," she said, "I suppose for once you're right. Nobody'd dare dump a pile of dirt on the roof without the landlord knowing about it. I guess I would just make myself ridiculous if I called and complained. But I'll tell you one thing, Lester. I'm going to keep my eye on what's happening around here."

"I'm sure of that," her husband said. "You always do."

Marcia Shapiro knocked at the Denton apartment. Mrs. Denton came to the door. Marcia peered past her.

"Why, that dirt isn't coming here at all. I thought you were going to use it on your geraniums."

"You'll find Melinda on the roof," Mrs. Denton said. "She's the one who's using all that dirt—she and Uncle Buck."

Marcia hurried up the stairs. Melinda was standing

near the gasoline engine which was turning a drum, winding up the cable that hauled the dirt from the street. When Melinda told her what she was planning, Marcia could hardly believe it.

"A pasture! Then you'll have a place to keep a horse."

"There's a lot of work to be done first. All Mr. O'Malley is going to do is dump the dirt here. We'll have to spread it around the roof ourselves."

"I'll help. We can get all the other girls in the building to help, if you'll let them come up and see your horse when you get it."

"I'm not sure how I'm going to get it. But I will somehow. And then you can help me take care of it and ride it and everything."

The winch and cable creaked most of the day. When evening came, there was a great pile of dirt on the roof. Melinda and Marcia regarded it.

"It sure is big," Marcia said. "It'll take us weeks to get it spread all around and leveled off."

"Maybe Mr. O'Malley can think of an easier way," Melinda suggested.

"Of course I know of an easier way than doing it by hand," O'Malley said, when they asked him. "The way to do it is to take a bulldozer and shove it where you want it to go. There'd be nothing to it—except for one thing. I don't see my way clear to hauling a bulldozer up on this roof."

"Then I guess we'll all just have to pitch in and shovel it," Melinda said. "Should we start now, Uncle Buck?"

Buck was stretched out in the hammock.

"Getting the dirt here was work enough for one day," he said. "It plumb wore me out, watching them machines work so hard."

"Should we get up early and start shoveling?"

"Let's see how it works out. I've got a notion it won't be as hard a job as it looks. To my way of thinking, the best way is to let nature give us a little help. Can you find me a piece of cardboard and a red crayon?"

Melinda didn't see how this would help distribute the dirt pile, but she went to the apartment and brought back the supplies. Buck carefully printed a sign.

"Boys Keep Out," it read. "Only Girls Allowed."

"Now you just tack this to the inside of the trapdoor where Harvey and his friends will see it," he said. "Then we'll all sleep late in the morning and see if boys are the same now as they were when I was one of them."

"If we don't allow them on the roof, I don't see how they can help, Mr. Denton," Marcia said.

"I didn't say we wouldn't allow them on the roof. All this sign does is tell them the girls don't want 'em around. That'll draw them like flies. And once we get a bunch of them boys up here, the laws of nature will take over."

Melinda had trouble sleeping late, but she stayed in bed as long as she could stand it. When she got dressed and went to the kitchen for breakfast, her mother and Buck were there. Harvey was nowhere around. She hurried through the meal and started out the door. Buck called her back.

"It don't do to rush old Mother Nature, girl. You just hang around here with me."

"Is Harvey up on the roof?"

"He walked out of here about the time I woke up. He didn't say where he was going."

"Then he might not be up there at all."

Buck only smiled and shrugged. Harvey came back to the apartment for lunch. He was not a boy who missed many meals. He sneaked into the bathroom and washed his hands without being told, which was unusual. He looked quite pleased with himself.

"What you been doing all morning, Son?" Buck asked him.

"Fooling around. Me and some of the other kids."

"Having fun, I trust."

"We was playing games—making stuff."

"Making what?" Melinda asked.

"You wouldn't understand. You're a girl."

Buck made her wait until late in the afternoon. Then they walked up the stairs to the trapdoor and opened it cautiously. Dozens of boys about Harvey's age were there. Some were making tunnels, some were making roads, some were digging. The pile was gone and the dirt was scattered all around the roof.

"Just like I told you," Uncle Buck said. "It pays to give nature a chance. It pays to turn a job like this over to an expert."

"And boys are experts on dirt?"

"Always have been. They can find it, and they can throw it around."

"And that sign you had me tack up brought them all up here?"

"You tell a boy he can't go somewhere, that's where he wants to go. That's another natural law."

Melinda closed the trapdoor softly behind her. She gave her great-uncle a hug.

"How do you know things like that? I would never have thought of it. Not even if I was lying in the hammock, looking at my mind's eye."

Uncle Buck waggled his beard at her.

"I'll tell you a secret," he said, "but don't let it go no further. You may not think of it to look at me, but underneath these whiskers and gray hair, I'm partly a small boy myself."

SIX

Mrs. Denton hadn't seemed to be paying any attention to what was going on up on the roof, but when Uncle Buck came back from the store with a burlap bag full of clover and timothy seed, she shoved open the trapdoor and prepared to go to work.

"Hand me that sack, Buck," she ordered. "Then you and Melinda take a couple of hoes and make me some rows. Put up a string from one edge of the roof to the other so you'll make the rows nice and straight."

"Now hold on there," Buck said. "I admit you know more about planting flowers and vegetables than me, but it sounds like you don't know much about how to plant grass."

"It grows from seeds, doesn't it? I know a lot about seeds."

"Then you ought to know you don't plant grass like you was planting petunias. What you do is sling the seed around in the loose dirt, scattering it in all directions. Let me show you."

Mrs. Denton watched him for a moment. Then she took over the job. Buck gave her the bag of seed without further argument. He stood aside, winking at Melinda.

"Now she's got it right. We couldn't ask for a better seed planter than your ma. She's got a green thumb."

"Does the seed really know who's planting it?"

"Maybe not. Still, there's some people like your ma who could plant stuff in concrete or a gravel pit and have it grow, while there's others who can go to all kinds of trouble and nothing'll sprout. When she gets a good start, you and me'll come along and spread a little fertilizer around. This ain't the richest pasture land in the world, so a little fertilizer won't do a bit of harm."

After Mrs. Denton had finished seeding the rooftop, she stood back and studied the situation.

"Now we've got to keep it moist and humid. What we ought to do is spread some burlap over it and keep it wet until the seed has sprouted. As long as we haven't got that much burlap, we'll have to do the next best thing. Melinda, you go down in our kitchen and open the window and reach out. I'll let down this length of garden hose. You can fasten it onto the faucet."

Melinda used the hose to keep the ground moist for several days. Each morning when she went up to the roof she looked anxiously for the first green sprout. Each morning she saw nothing but the expanse of moist dirt. But on the fifth day, a few tiny shafts of green appeared. By the next evening the grass had sprouted from one side of the roof to the other.

Uncle Buck put up a sign to warn people not to walk on it. Melinda kept watering the new pasture with the garden hose and before long the grass was growing vigorously. Marcia Shapiro put her head through the doorway and looked at it admiringly. Kermit Hofreitz paid a visit to the roof and said he would never have believed it if he hadn't seen it. Sylvester Denton appeared with a bucket in his hand.

"This is a fine pasture you've got started," he told Melinda. "But something's missing. What it needs is some worms."

"So you can come up and dig them when you want to go fishing?"

"Well, I admit I did have that in the back of my mind. But the worms'll help aerate the soil. Isn't that right, Buck?"

"Sure it is. Go ahead and dump them on our pasture. They ought to like living here better than living in a bucket."

By the first of June, the grass was six inches tall. A few dandelions were mixed with it. Mrs. Denton was all for pulling them out, but Buck stopped her.

"I know they're a pest and a nuisance. But living in the city this way, a man gets downright hungry for the sight of them. You got to admit they're pretty."

"Yes, they are," Charlene Denton said. "But you won't like it when they spread."

"The horse will keep them down," Melinda told her. "That is, when I get a horse. Isn't it about time to start thinking about getting one, Uncle Buck?"

"Not yet, it ain't. How you going to have a horse up here? This is nothing but an open field. A horse don't belong in an open field."

"You mean we need a fence?"

"We need a horse fence. It's got to be made out of white-painted boards."

"I shouldn't think a horse would try to get out of this pasture," Mrs. Denton said. "Most horses would be smart enough to know it wouldn't be a good idea to step off the side of a building twelve stories high. What do you need a white board fence for?"

"We need a white board fence because that's the kind

they had around the horse pastures back home," Buck said, and that settled the argument.

Melinda helped measure the pasture and figure out how many posts and boards would be needed. Buck took her figures and made some calculations of his own with a pencil and paper. Then he shook his head.

"That many boards is going to be mighty expensive. I don't see my way clear to buying them."

It turned out, however, that Rusty O'Malley was tearing down a wooden building and was willing to let them have the boards and enough two-by-fours to use for posts. The winch was put back in place. The cable snaked down from the roof to the sidewalk. Mrs. Pontey looked out of her window just as a pile of scrap lumber was being hoisted past.

"What are they doing up there now?" she demanded. "I'd give a lot to know what's going on."

"You could go up on the roof and ask," her husband suggested.

"And let everybody know I was curious? No, sir. I wouldn't give them the satisfaction. But this sort of nonsense has gone just about far enough."

When all the boards were on the roof, Melinda and Buck started putting up the fence. The sound of the hammering brought Harvey to investigate. He stayed to help. Sylvester Denton was already on the roof, working on plans for a catapult to shoot a fishing line from there to the river. He put his invention aside and started hammering nails in the boards. A girl about Melinda's age climbed through the trapdoor.

"I'm Mary Ruth O'Malley. My father said you wouldn't mind if I came up to watch."

Uncle Buck waggled his beard at her.

"Grab hold of the end of this here board, young lady.

We don't need watchers. We need fence builders. You ever built a white board fence for a horse?"

"No, I never did. But if it's for a horse, I'm ready to learn."

With so many hands, it didn't take long to put up the fence. There were plenty of fence painters, too, with Mary and Melinda swinging brushes, Harvey and his father mixing the paint and carrying it to where it was needed, and with Uncle Buck lying in the hammock with his eyes closed, supervising the entire operation. When the afternoon was over, the fence gleamed in the setting sun, every board in place and painted.

"Now that's more like it," Buck said. "This here pasture is beginning to look like it did when I first saw it in my mind's eye."

"It'd look a lot better with a frog pond over in one corner," Harvey said.

"It isn't bad," Sylvester said. "But when I get my fishing catapult ready, it'll be a lot more useful."

"I think it's beautiful," Melinda said. "But it's awfully empty, isn't it, Mary Ruth?"

"It does need something," Rusty O'Malley's daughter agreed.

"It needs a horse," Melinda said. "Uncle Buck, when is the deal you're working on going to come through? I've been waiting and waiting."

"Now it don't do no good to rush nature, girls. Nature don't like to be hurried."

"We've got our pasture. We've got our fence. But it doesn't mean a thing without a horse. Isn't it time yet?"

Buck edged away. He had some things he wanted to attend to down in the apartment, he said. Melinda wouldn't be put off. She took hold of his arm.

"Please, Uncle Buck. I've just got to know. When am I going to get my horse?"

"And where?" Mary Ruth said. "Also, how?"

Buck sighed. He ran his hand through his bushy white hair. He fidgeted back and forth. Then he motioned to the girls to follow him.

"If I've got to tell you, then I'll tell you. But let's go somewhere that Harvey and my nephew won't hear. It's one of them things that I'd just as soon not too many people knew about until we see how it all works out."

seven

When the two girls and Uncle Buck got to the Denton kitchen, he walked over to the cupboard and brought out a large box of cereal. He held it up.

"As you may have noticed," he said, "I've been eating Buckwheat Roasties every morning lately instead of my usual breakfast of flapjacks with country sausage."

"I did notice that," Melinda told him. "But what's that got to do with what we came down here from the pasture to talk about?"

"Have you ever happened to taste a spoonful of Buckwheat Roasties?"

"I did once," Mary Ruth said. "It tasted icky."

"I tried it day before yesterday," Melinda said. "What do they make it out of, buckwheat straw?"

"I wouldn't be at all surprised," Buck said. "And not a very good grade of buckwheat straw, at that. Still, I want you to know that I've eaten seventeen boxes full of Buckwheat Roasties since I started."

"That's very interesting," Melinda said. "But we were supposed to come down here and talk about a horse."

"I'm leading up to that, gradual like. What would you say if I was to tell you that this here cereal might lead the way to our getting a full-blooded Arabian colt worth five thousand dollars?"

"It will?" Melinda cried. "How wonderful! I'm sorry I said anything against it. I don't care if it does taste like old straw, if it gets us a horse."

"Now I didn't exactly say it would get us one. I just said it might. Take a look at this fine print on the back of the cereal box, right below the place where I've cut out the box top."

Melinda and Mary Ruth grabbed the box and read where Buck was pointing.

"A contest," Melinda said. "You're expecting to win us a horse in a contest? But there must be millions of other entries, Uncle Buck."

"Not as many as you might think. The way I figure it, not many people would be willing to eat seventeen boxes of Buckwheat Roasties for as small a sum as five thousands dollars. One box would be about the limit for anybody except an old codger who was doing his level best to win a full-blooded Arabian colt for his niece."

Melinda told her great-uncle she appreciated his sacrifice in giving up flapjacks and sausage for a breakfast food like Buckwheat Roasties. But she wasn't quite able to keep the disappointment out of her voice. Buck put his arm around her shoulders.

"I know I don't have much chance of winning, girl. But somebody's got to take first prize. Even second prize wouldn't be bad—they give you a choice between two thousand, five hundred dollars and a trip to Europe, and I figure I'll just take the money and then we can buy our own horse. By sending in seventeen box tops, I ought to have as good a chance as anybody."

"I'll help," Melinda said. "With both of us eating Buckwheat Roasties, we'll get more entries."

"It's too late now. The contest closed last week. I thought of suggesting that you and Harvey help me eat the stuff, but after I'd tasted it I just didn't have the heart. It can't do much harm to me, after all these years. But you two shouldn't eat it. It might stunt your growth."

After dinner, Harvey carried his plate out to the kitchen. He noticed the box of cereal on the counter. He picked it up to put it away and saw that the top was missing.

"Who's been entering contests around here?" he asked.

"Uncle Buck," Melinda told him. "But he doesn't like to talk about it."

"Is that how he was going to get you a horse? Boy, adults get some funny ideas sometimes. I used to enter all kinds of contests when I was younger. I never won a thing."

"That doesn't prove anything."

"Oh, no? Well, every single kid I know enters contests and I never knew one who got a prize. It's a waste of time and postage."

Uncle Buck had walked into the kitchen while they were talking.

"Maybe so," he said, his voice dejected. "But I felt like I had to do something, and I couldn't think of any other way to get the horse Melinda wanted. I guess I was just wasting my time, like you say."

"I appreciate it, Uncle Buck," Melinda said. "Besides, maybe you will win."

"Not much chance, I guess. It's just that I had the feeling that you wanted a horse so bad maybe we'd be lucky. And then I guess I thought maybe the laws of nature might help out a little, too."

"Laws of nature?" Harvey said, scornfully. "I don't see what they've got to do with winning a box-top contest."

"It's a law of nature, boy, that when you have a good piece of pasture land surrounded by a white board fence, a horse has just naturally got to appear there, sooner or later. I thought I'd give Mother Nature a chance to take care of the shortage of horses in our pasture by entering the contest."

"Nobody I know ever wins one," Harvey said. "Even Brains Jankowski, who lives over in the next block, never wins. And he's the smartest kid in the fifth grade, aside from me."

The doorbell sounded. Melinda spoke into the tube that was connected to a speaker in the apartment-house entryway.

"Denton residence. Who is it, please?"

"Someone with a message for Hezekiah Denton," a man's voice said. "Is he in?"

"We don't have anybody by that name here," Melinda said, but Uncle Buck pushed her aside.

"That's me. I don't generally admit it, but it's what my mama called me. What is it, mister? This is Buck Denton—I mean Hezekiah."

"I'm Les Poulting from the Buckwheat Roasties company. May I come up?"

"Buckwheat Roasties!" Buck took a step back. "Yes, sir. Oh, my, yes. Come up and tell us what this is all about."

While they were waiting for Poulting to get from the street level to the twelfth floor, Melinda and Harvey and Uncle Buck kept telling each other not to get excited.

"You got to remember that he might just be coming to tell me I've lost," Buck said.

"The company wouldn't send him here to do that," Melinda insisted. "They wouldn't send him around to see you unless you'd won. In a big contest like this, they wouldn't go to the trouble to notify all the losers."

"You never can tell. There probably aren't many of us who've sent in seventeen entries. Maybe they just want to meet a man who's survived after eating that much buck-wheat straw."

There was a knock at the door. Melinda got to it first. Les Poulting swept inside the apartment, wearing a big smile.

"Are you Hezekiah Denton, sir?" he asked Harvey.

"I'm the party you're after," Buck said, waggling his beard nervously.

"You are? Well, well. You must excuse the mistake, sir. Mostly we get entries from younger cereal eaters, the ones who grow big and strong and husky from brimming bowls filled with crunchy Buckwheat Roasties."

"I suppose there's no rule against people my age entering your contest?" Buck asked.

"None at all, sir. A man is never too old to eat Buckwheat Roasties. Judging from the number of box tops you sent in, it must be your favorite breakfast cereal."

"I never tasted nothing like it," Buck said. "Yes, sir, I can truthfully say that there's nothing like Buckwheat Roasties. In fact, if I hadn't found out what it tasted like for myself, I'd never have believed it."

"Thank you very much, sir. We're always happy to meet a satisfied customer."

"Oh, it don't take more than a spoonful or two to satisfy me."

"Well, now, I'm glad to hear you like them so much," Poulting said, beaming. "But I suppose you want to know why I'm here. I won't keep you in suspense." He reached out and shook Buck's hand. "Congratulations, Hezekiah. You are a winner in the nationwide Buckwheat Roasties contest."

Melinda had been holding her breath since Les Poulting walked through the door. Now she couldn't contain herself any longer. She hugged Uncle Buck and she would have hugged Harvey if he hadn't seen her coming and ducked out of the way.

"What'll we name him, Uncle Buck? When will we get him? Do you think he'll like our pasture? Do you suppose he'll—"

But Les Poulting was holding up his hand and shaking his head.

"Now, now, young lady. Let's not jump to conclusions. I didn't say that Hezekiah had won first prize. That distinction was achieved by a rancher in southern Arizona. He will add our five-thousand-dollar Arabian colt to his stable of twenty-three horses. But even though Hezekiah did not win first place, he has a great treat in store for him."

"So it's only second," Buck said. "Well, I'll just take the two thousand, five hundred dollars instead of the trip, if you don't mind. I'd like to see Europe, all right. But I'll get more enjoyment out of watching Melinda's face when I use the money to go out and buy us a fine little filly that will—"

"I'm afraid you didn't win second, either," Poulting said. "The second-place prize of a trip to Europe went to a stewardess on an international airline. She will certainly enjoy the journey if she ever gets time off from her job of flying between New York and Paris. But I don't want to keep you in suspense any longer. It is my pleasure and privilege to be able to inform you, Hezekiah, that the judges have picked one of your entries for third place in the contest. My very hearty congratulations."

"Third?" Buck said. "I don't seem to recollect much

about third—I was thinking mainly of first or second. Still, I guess third's a lot better than nothing."

"I should certainly say it is, sir," Poulting assured him. "In fact, if it were me, I'd prefer it. A trip to Europe would be pleasant. but when it's over what have you got? A five-thousand-dollar Arabian colt would be nice to have, but keeping a horse is a lot of trouble. For myself, if I were a contest winner, third place is the one I would have chosen to win."

"Let's see now," Buck said. "There was a prize worth five thousand dollars and a prize worth two thousand five hundred. So I figure third prize ought to be worth—"

"It's rather hard to put a monetary value on buying happiness, isn't it?" Poulting said. "There are other things than money that are far more important. and here is one of them, sir. May I present to you this certificate, signed not only by the president of our company but by the genius who invented the cereal himself. He took time off from his busy task of gathering up buckwheat straw in Nebraska just to put his name down."

Buck took the piece of paper and stared at it.

"This is third prize?"

"And a wonderful prize it is, Hezekiah. It not only testifies that you have placed third in our contest, but it entitles you to a lifetime supply of Buckwheat Roasties. For as long as you live, you need never be without the special flavor and goodness of our breakfast food. I envy you. Truly I do."

Buck's mind was working furiously. He ran his hand through his hair. He waggled his beard. Then he squinted up his eyes with the air of a man who has managed to discover a way of turning grim defeat into victory.

"As long as you enjoy Buckwheat Roasties so much," he said, "I've got a little proposition for you. I'll sell you this here piece of paper for the price of a horse. Then you won't ever have to be without your favorite cereal."

Les Poulting took a step toward the door.

"No, thanks," he said. "The lifetime supply of our product is yours. I always have flapjacks and country sausage for breakfast myself."

eight

Melinda got up early the next morning and climbed the stairs to the roof. The grass was growing taller. A mild breeze sent ripples across it. She walked across the pasture and leaned on the top board of the fence, looking down on the neighboring roofs. She didn't hear her father approach until he was close behind her.

"You're up early," he said. "Why the solemn face?"

"I feel so sorry for Uncle Buck. He was so disappointed."

Sylvester Denton smiled down at her.

"And you weren't, I suppose. I heard all about what happened from Harvey. It was too bad, but it could have been worse. Suppose Buck had won a lifetime supply of Buckwheat Roasties for the entire family instead of just for himself. Then we'd all have to eat it."

Melinda knew he was trying to cheer her up, but she didn't feel like joking about what had happened. She turned back to lean on the fence again.

"I guess I'll never have a horse, Dad. I guess I'll just have to appreciate what I do have—all this green grass and everything. But the pasture looks so empty."

"I'll tell you something," her father said, putting down

the tools he was carrying. "Your great-uncle isn't the only one who's been giving this problem a little thought. I've been asking around among all my fishing buddies. You'd be surprised at how much good advice you can get while you're sitting around, waiting for the fish to bite. I just might have a suggestion about how you can get a horse—and you won't have to send in seventeen box tops, either."

"You really mean it, Dad?"

"I don't know whether it'll work out. But why don't we take a drive up north to Putnam County today? There's a fishing buddy of mine who lives up there by the name of Maybe Carstairs—they call him Maybe because it's so hard to get a yes or no answer out of him. 'Maybe yes' he'll say or 'maybe no.' I was thinking maybe we'd go see Maybe."

"But don't you have to go to work?"

"I'm taking a day off. I was planning to come up here and work on my fish-line catapult, but that'll keep. We'll take our poles along and see if we can work in a little fishing, so the trip won't be wasted even if Maybe turns out to be no help to us."

"Does this Mr. Carstairs have a horse?"

"He used to have one, I hear. He was going into the horse-raising business, only he could never quite make up his mind whether to do it or not. 'Maybe I will,' he told me the last time I fished with him. 'Then again, maybe I won't.' He might have sold the mare by now. But even if he has, he might know somebody who's got a horse that would like to live twelve stories up in the air."

Melinda ran downstairs and woke Uncle Buck, who cheered up at once when he heard what was planned. Harvey wanted to go along, too. They got in Sylvester's old sedan and headed north on the West Side Highway. After about an hour of driving, they turned off the main road and went back into the hills. Within another hour, they were on a dirt road that led to a small farmhouse built alongside a brook that tumbled down through the Highlands toward the Hudson River, several miles away. Maybe Carstairs came out to greet them. He was wearing old clothes and carrying a shovel.

"You're lucky you caught me home, Sylvester," he said. "I was thinking some of driving over to Fishkill and buying groceries. 'Maybe I'll do it,' I said to myself. But then I decided maybe tomorrow would be time enough, so I started out to do some ditching around the barn. But I wasn't sure where the ditch should go—I thought at first maybe it ought to go on the downslope, where it'd carry the runoff, but as I got to studying the lay of the land I wondered if maybe it ought to go someplace else."

"What we ought to do is go fishing and think the matter over," Sylvester said. "Only first, we thought we'd take a look at that horse of yours—if you've still got her, that is."

"Oh, I've still got Marshmallow. You may remember, I was going to start raising horses. But I wasn't sure it'd be worth all the trouble. Maybe I'd make me some money and maybe I wouldn't. You know how it is."

"Can we see her?" Melinda asked. "Marshmallow is a nice name for a horse."

"I was going to change it," Maybe said. "But I never got around to it. Sure, you can go on out to the barn if you want to. She'll be hanging around there somewhere, eating grass."

Melinda and Uncle Buck went to the pasture near the barn, with Harvey trailing along. Marshmallow was a chestnut-colored horse with a placid look. She raised her head long enough to find out who was coming, then went back to cropping the grass.

"She's not a bad-looking animal," Buck said. "You like her, Melinda?"

"Oh, yes. I think she's beautiful."

"You think every horse is beautiful," Harvey said, scornfully.

"That's because they are. But Marshmallow has such a friendly look."

They walked over. Melinda reached up and patted the side of the mare's neck. Uncle Buck opened her mouth and looked at her teeth. Then he walked around her at a little distance, studying her.

"She's no young filly. Eight or ten years old, by my guess. She looks nice and healthy, though."

"All she does is eat," Harvey said. "I don't see what fun it is to stand around eating grass all day."

"That's what horses do most of the time, if you let 'em," Buck said. "She's well filled out."

"She's fat, if you ask me," Harvey said.

"She is not," Melinda told him. "She's just right. Aren't you, Marshmallow? Feel how soft her nose is, Uncle Buck. It's like velvet."

When they walked down to the brook to talk to Carstairs, Sylvester had already caught three fair-sized trout and Maybe had nearly decided where to start fishing.

"They might be biting over there by the ripples," he said, studying the situation. "On the other hand, maybe this is the kind of day when it'd be better to fish deep. Maybe I ought to try the pool."

"We like Marshmallow, Mr. Carstairs," Melinda said. "Is she for sale?"

"You'll have to excuse my grand-neice, Maybe," Buck said. "She doesn't know much about the horse-tradin' business. She doesn't know that if you're interested in buying a horse you always start out by telling the owner that it's kind of a sorry-looking beast."

"Maybe she is kind of lazy," Carstairs admitted. "On the other hand, maybe she isn't—I never have really asked her to do much except eat. She does that pretty well."

"Yes, she seems to do right well at eating," Buck said. "Must be a lot of trouble and expense."

"I don't know as she's even for sale," Maybe said. "If she was, I'd have to have at least five hundred dollars for a fine animal like that."

"She's certainly worth that much," Melinda said. "Of course, we don't happen to have it, but—"

Uncle Buck was pulling at her arm. She followed him to one side, out of earshot of the others.

"Buying a horse is kind of a special type of transaction, girl. The fellow selling it always starts high and the fellow buying it starts low and then, if everything goes right, they meet somewheres in the middle. But if you keep telling old Maybe what a fine animal he's got, you're going to spoil the dickering for both of us."

"But I've just got to have her, Uncle Buck. Now that I've seen her and touched her soft nose and everything—"

"And I'm going to try to get her for you. But I'll never be able to do it unless you keep quiet."

Melinda said she would try. Buck walked back to where the two men were fishing. He said that Marshmallow wasn't exactly what they'd had in mind—what they really had been considering, he told Maybe, was a five-thousand-dollar Arab palomino.

"But as a favor to an old fishing buddy of my nephew's," Buck went on, "we might see our way clear to taking her off your hands for a fair price. Say fifty bucks."

"Fifty dollars!" Carstairs nearly dropped his fishing

pole. "You're offering fifty dollars for a horse that might have won first prize at the international exposition?"

"I didn't know she was entered."

"She wasn't. I was thinking about entering her, though. I thought maybe I'd put her in my truck and haul her down there and have her win first prize. But on the other hand, I thought maybe it'd be too much trouble, and by the time I'd decided what to do about it the show was over. But if she'd been in the international exposition, maybe she'd have won."

"And maybe she wouldn't."

"I'll tell you what I'll do, Buck. Instead of asking five hundred dollars, maybe I'd take four hundred."

"And maybe I could see fit to raise my offer to seventy-five. Providing we decide we want her. Is she trained for riding?"

"She surely is. The fellow I bought her from used to ride her all over the country. Matter of fact, I've been considering maybe entering her in the Kentucky Derby or one of those races. Maybe she'd win."

"She's a mite old for that," Buck said. "Has she ever won any races?"

"She's never lost any."

"On account of she's never run in any?"

"Maybe you could say that. I'll tell you what—I might come down to three hundred, seeing as how you're a relative of a fishing buddy. But not a dime less."

"And I might raise my offer to a hundred," Buck said, winking at Melinda. "And not a dime more."

By the time the dickering was over, Sylvester had a fine collection of fish, Harvey had made friends with several frogs, and Melinda had wandered off to tell Marshmallow how pleasant it would be to live on a rooftop. Buck rounded them up and told them it was time to head back to the city. Melinda started to ask how soon they could get the horse but her great-uncle motioned to her to be quiet until they were riding back down the country road and Carstairs was no longer able to listen.

"You did get her, Uncle Buck?" Melinda asked. "I don't think I can stand it if you didn't."

"I haven't had as much fun in a long time. I'd nearly forgot how fine it is to do some horse tradin'."

"The last I heard, Maybe wanted three hundred dollars," Sylvester said. "Did he come down any from that?"

"Oh, he come down a little. He won't admit it, but he's getting mighty tired of watching that horse eat. We finally settled on what I consider a pretty good price—a hundred fifty-three dollars and thirty cents."

"That's kind of an odd figure."

"I don't see as it is, Sylvester. We decided the horse was worth a hundred and fifty and it'll cost Maybe three dollars and thirty cents worth of gas for his old truck to deliver her to the apartment. There's only one catch to all this, though."

"There can't be," Melinda said. "There just can't be a catch to it."

"But there is," Buck said. "The catch is that we don't have the hundred fifty-three dollars, although I guess if we pooled our spare money we could raise the thirty cents."

nine

The Denton family held a council in the living room after dinner to discuss how to get the money to buy the horse.

"According to our budget," Sylvester said, "my salary and our bills always come out exactly even each month. I'm rather proud of that record. In most families I know, there's a deficit. However, it doesn't leave much margin for buying horses."

"I have five dollars put away," Mrs. Denton said. "I'd planned to use it when next year's seed catalogs came out, but I'm willing to put it in the kitty. It isn't much, but it's a start."

"I can see my way clear to buying a third of the horse," Uncle Buck said. "For the last sixty years, I've been putting money aside for my old age, but it looks like I won't need it for a long time yet. So I'll invest my life savings of fifty dollars in Melinda's horse."

"You two make me ashamed of myself," Sylvester declared. "If Charlene can give up her flower seeds and Buck can give up his old age, I guess I can do without that new fishing rod. I've got forty-five dollars hidden away and you can have it."

"I can chip in the three dollars and thirty cents to pay for Maybe's gasoline," Harvey said. "Brains Jankowski said he'll give me three dollars and a quarter for twenty-five of my frogs, and I have a nickel in cash."

"I can't let you sell all your frogs," Melinda said. "I know how much they mean to you."

"Who's talking about selling all of them? I'm just going to get rid of twenty-five. I'll still have fifty-three left."

"Well, that brings us up to a hundred three dollars and thirty cents, counting Harvey's nickel in cash," Buck said. "All we need is another fifty."

"I don't suppose Maybe would come down any more on his price?" Sylvester asked.

"Nope. Besides, dickering's one thing, but paying less than a hundred fifty-three dollars and thirty cents for that horse would be cheating. The way I look at it, Marshmallow's worth that much."

"She's worth anything she costs," Melinda said. "I have five dollars I got for my birthday. But we'll still need another forty-five dollars. I guess Mr. Carstairs will just have to keep the horse until we get it."

"We mustn't wait too long," Buck said. "Maybe's the kind of fellow who changes his mind easy. Besides, he's getting mighty tired of seeing Marshmallow stand around and eat."

"I could borrow the money," Sylvester said.

But Melinda shook her head.

"I'm the one who wants the horse most, Dad. It's up to me to figure out some way to get the rest of the money."

The next morning, she walked up to the roof to think about it. Marcia joined her. They sat in the grass to talk about what they could do.

"If you had the horse, you could charge kids a quarter

each to ride her," Marcia said. "But you don't have the horse."

"Maybe I could get jobs baby-sitting or running errands. But it'd take too long to raise the money that way."

"Then what are you going to do, Melinda?"

"I'm going to do what my Great-Uncle Buck would do, if he wasn't still downstairs sleeping." Melinda stood up and squared her shoulders. "I'm going to walk right over there to that hammock. I'm going to stretch out in it. Then I'm going to look at the problem with my mind's eye."

"You ought to waggle your beard, too," Marcia said. "I've noticed your uncle always waggles his beard in a situation like this. But maybe it'll work without it."

The solution came to Melinda almost as soon as she leaned back and closed her eyes. It was so simple she wondered why she hadn't thought of it before. She sat up so quickly she almost fell out of the hammock.

"Marcia, would you buy a share in a horse? How much would you pay to be able to say a horse was partly yours?"

"Three dollars and eighty-six cents. That happens to be exactly how much I have in the bank on top of my dresser."

"Do you think some of the other girls would like to own part of a horse?"

"Sure they would. Melinda, that's a wonderful idea."

"And I got it without having a beard to waggle back and forth, too. Let's draw up some official papers and go out and see how it works."

The plan to sell shares in Marshmallow worked very well. Melinda got her five dollars and Marcia hurried downstairs for her three dollars and eigthty-six cents. The two girls signed documents showing they were part owners of Marshmallow. Then they got more writing paper and drew up some more documents. Mary Ruth O'Malley, who got a weekly allowance from her father, bought twelve dollars and eighteen cents' worth of the horse. Karen Hofstetter, who lived on the third floor, bought a four-dollar share. Nancy Gormley, whose father ran the delicatessen down the block, chipped in six dollars and a half and her younger sister, Barbara, bought three dollars' worth of Marshmallow. Eve Schultz from the seventh floor took a seven-dollar-and-twenty-eight-cent share. Jean Kauffman and Isabel Thomas, who always did everything together, each bought four-dollar shares. The girls sat in a circle on the rooftop pasture and added up the money they'd raised. It came to forty-nine dollars and eighty-two cents—nearly but not quite enough. As they were discussing the shortage, Brains Jankowski stuck his head through the trapdoor.

"I'm looking for Harvey. He's going to sell me twenty-five frogs."

"Why don't you buy a share in a horse, too?" Marcia suggested. "You get more for your money if you buy a horse than if you buy a frog."

"But I like frogs."

"You're going to have trouble feeding that many frogs," Melinda said. "You'll have to spend all your time catching flies. Of course, if you were one of Marshmallow's co-owners, you could hang around the stable. There's usually a fine supply of flies around a stable."

Brains regarded the girls with suspicion.

"How much would it cost me? After I pay Harvey for the frogs, I won't have much left."

Melinda studied the sheet of figures in front of her. "You can have the right to catch all the flies you want to in our stable for eighteen cents," she said. "That's all we need to raise our fifty dollars."

Brains admitted that the price was right. He dug down into his pocket and came up with eighteen pennies.

Sylvester drove Buck and Melinda to the Carstairs' place after he got home from work. They found Maybe trying to make up his mind what to fix for dinner—he wasn't sure whether to have hamburger patties with sweet corn or broiled brook trout with french fries. When Buck said they'd come to buy the horse, Maybe wasn't sure whether he ought to sell her after all.

"Maybe I should and maybe I shouldn't. On the one hand, there's something to be said for getting rid of her. On the other—"

"Now look here, Maybe," Buck interrupted. "We made a deal."

"But maybe you won't want to go through with it when I tell you something about Marshmallow I forgot to mention the other day."

"What's that?" Buck asked, suspiciously.

"It's kind of personal. Why don't you and me take a little walk and talk about it? Then if you still want to buy her, I guess maybe it'll be all right."

When Uncle Buck and Carstairs had gone, Melinda and her father looked at each other. Sylvester put his arm around his daughter.

"Now don't be too disappointed if it turns out we don't get the horse, honey. As long as we've got the money, we can always buy a horse somewhere."

"But not for a bargain price like this one. Besides, Marshmallow wants me to have her. I can tell by the way she looked at me when we drove in."

When the two men got back from their stroll, Uncle

Buck was grinning. He winked at Melinda.

"What's wrong with Marshmallow?" she asked him.

"Not a thing, girl. Of course, it's all how you look at it. Some folks might think getting two horses for the price of one wasn't much of a bargain. She's going to have a colt."

"I wasn't sure the last time you were out," Maybe said. "I thought maybe she would and maybe she wouldn't. But Doc Amherst, the vet, happened to stop by for some fishing yesterday and he had a look at her. He says it ought to happen next spring. Of course, if you want to call off the deal—"

Maybe let the sentence dangle there. He was not a man who reached decisions easily, but he made up his mind without having to stop and look into the matter further when he saw the expression on Melinda's face. He knew further talk would be a waste of time. He patted her hand.

"I guess having the colt on its way will make it even better, won't it?"

Melinda nodded. She didn't trust herself to say anything. Buck cleared his throat.

"Then I guess it's settled," he said. "I guess Melinda's been wishing all her life for a colt, and now it looks like she'll have one, with a mama horse to go with it."

"She really wants the colt, doesn't she?" Maybe said.

"You bet she does. There ain't enough money in the world to buy her anything she wants more. But the price is still one hundred and fifty bucks."

"Plus three dollars and thirty cents for the gas," Maybe said. "And I just hope you know what you're doing, taking Marshmallow to live twelve stories up in the air in New York City."

ten

It was late afternoon when Carstairs drove up in front of Whetstone Manor with Marshmallow. Several passersby were tempted to stop and look at the rare sight of a large mare placidly chewing hay in the back of an open truck on the city street. But then they remembered they were New Yorkers and not supposed to be astonished at anything, so they walked on.

Melinda was waiting on the sidewalk. She'd been waiting there since 6:30 A.M., with ten minutes off for lunch. Harvey was watching from the window. He alerted the other Dentons, who hurried downstairs to discuss how to get the horse to the roof.

"It isn't my problem," Maybe said cheerfully. "All I agreed to do was deliver her. From now on, Marshmallow's yours."

"Isn't she beautiful?" Melinda asked her mother. "Isn't she just as beautiful as I told you she was?"

"She's a very nice-looking animal. A very big one, too."

"She does look bigger than when she was out in the country," Sylvester said. "You given any thought to how we get her up to the pasture, Buck?"

Whetstone Manor
NO
PARKING
TAXI

"I've given it a lot of thought. I haven't thought of any good answer, though."

"Maybe I ought to get her down off the truck, seeing as how I'm in a no-parking zone," Carstairs said. "If you fellows will give me a hand, we'll lay these boards from the tailgate down to the sidewalk so we can lead her down."

Marshmallow hesitated about trusting her weight to the boards, but Melinda spoke gently to her and the horse allowed her to take hold of the halter and lead her off the truck. Carstairs took the money they gave him. Several dollars of it was in pennies, but he didn't bother to count it. He jumped back behind the wheel and started the engine.

"Good luck, folks," he said. "Don't worry about Marshmallow. Maybe she'll fit in the elevator. Then again, maybe she won't."

The truck drove off, with Carstairs waving to them and laughing.

"Yes, maybe she'll fit in the elevator," Sylvester said, dubiously. "But I'm inclined to doubt it."

Melinda led Marshmallow into the apartment-house lobby and pressed the up button of the elevator. The larger of the two cages arrived first. Melinda started to lead the horse inside, but Buck stopped her. He whipped out a tape measure and checked the dimensions of the elevator. Then he measured Marshmallow. He shook his head.

"She'd almost fit, standing crossways. And she probably could get in if she'd set down and hold up her front legs. But everything considered, I guess we'd better try the stairs. I'd hate to get her stuck inside the elevator. Some of the other tenants might get sore."

"Especially Mrs. Pontey," Sylvester said. "That old biddy has been going around complaining about us putting dirt on the roof and raising grass up there. It's hard to say what she might do if she pushed the button for the elevator and came face to face with a full-grown horse."

"It'd be quite a shock for the horse, too," Buck pointed out.

Melinda led Marshmallow across the lobby. The mare looked around, curious about her new surroundings. She started to walk over and nibble on a potted palm tree that was in one corner of the room, but Melinda persuaded her to walk through the door and start climbing the stairway to the second floor.

Everything went remarkably well for a while. Marshmallow had never climbed apartment-house stairs before, but she was willing to try. She walked up to the second-floor landing cheerfully enough, pausing there to admire the view out of the window. Then, at Melinda's urging, the horse climbed to the third-floor level and, more reluctantly, to the fourth. Then she planted her front feet and refused to budge.

"I don't think she wants to go any higher, Uncle Buck," Melinda said. "What'll we do?"

"I thought this might happen," Harvey said. "I came prepared." He reached into his pocket and pulled out a large frog. "Stand back now. When she sees this, she's liable to run all the way to the twelfth floor."

"Marshmallow isn't afraid of an old frog," Melinda said. "And if she is, I don't want her scared."

"You want her to climb the rest of the stairs, don't you? Get a good grip on the halter, now. I'm going to turn him loose."

Harvey set the frog on the floor near Marshmallow's front feet. The horse put her head down and looked at the frog. The frog gathered its hind legs underneath its plump body and looked up at the horse. Then it gave a mighty leap toward the stairs leading to the next floor.

"Now look what your horse has done," Harvey said. "She's scared my frog. He's getting away."

The frog took the stairs three at a time. Marshmallow's curiosity was aroused. She followed, keeping a few steps behind, with Melinda clinging to the halter. The horse chased the frog to the sixth-floor landing. Then Harvey's pet crouched in a corner and refused to move. Marshmallow stopped. She took a final look at the frog, lost interest and started gazing thoughtfully out of the window.

"She wants some grass," Melinda said. "Hold her, Uncle Buck. I'll run upstairs to the pasture and get some."

It seemed like a good idea. Melinda returned with a handful of grass and held it in front of Marshmallow. The horse reached out for it. Melinda took a step back, moving toward the next flight of stairs. Marshmallow set her feet and refused to leave.

"She wants an apple," Mrs. Denton said. "She was eating hay in the truck so she isn't willing to go to much trouble for a handful of grass, but she'll probably move for an apple. I'll go get one."

Marshmallow took a bite of the apple eagerly enough. Mrs. Denton pulled it away and tried to persuade the horse to resume climbing the stairs. Marshmallow went back to looking out of the window.

"She's never been up this high before," Harvey said. "She doesn't want to go any higher. It looks to me like you've got a twelve-story pasture and a six-story horse."

"Well, we've got to get her out of here," Sylvester said. "This is Mrs. Pontey's floor. She's liable to come popping in on us to find out what's going on, and then where'll we be?"

"Why don't you and me push from behind while Melinda pulls on her halter?" Buck suggested.

The men pushed as hard as they could. Marshmallow ignored them.

"I suppose it wouldn't do any good to get my fish line and dangle some bait in front of her," Sylvester said, wearily.

"Marshmallow's smarter than a fish, Dad," Melinda told him. "Maybe she likes potted plants—she was trying to get at the one in the lobby. Mom, do you suppose—?"

"Now there's where I draw the line," Mrs. Denton said. "She's a nice horse, although a little stubborn. I'm in favor of doing anything within reason to get her the rest of the way to the roof. But when it comes to feeding her my geraniums and begonias, I draw the line."

"I wish I had something to give her to make her change her mind," Buck said. "But I don't really have anything except a lifetime supply of—" He stopped. He waggled his beard back and forth. "Hey, maybe that's the answer."

"Maybe what's the answer?" Melinda asked. But her great-uncle was already bounding up the stairway, his white hair in disarray.

He returned in a few minutes with his arms full of boxes of Buckwheat Roasties. He opened one. He sprinkled some of the cereal into his hand. He held it under Marshmallow's nose.

She tasted it hesitantly. Then she lunged forward. Buck leaped back to get out of her way, spilling the rest of the opened package. Marshmallow put down her head and ate up every crumb.

"She likes it!" Melinda said. "Give her some more."

"Gladly," Buck said. "But she's going to have to climb to get it."

He opened another box of the cereal and made a trail of Buckwheat Roasties. It led up the stairway to the seventh floor, then to the eighth. Marshmallow clambered up the steps behind him, eating it almost as fast as he could put it down. Buck kept ahead of her to the tenth floor, where she nearly caught him. But he jumped nimbly out of her way and ran on up the stairs and out of the trapdoor, leaving a trail of Buckwheat Roasties behind him. Marshmallow reached the roof almost as soon as he did and looked anxiously around. Then she headed toward him. He held her off with one hand and dumped the rest of the cereal in the grass at her feet.

"We did it," Melinda said, out of breath. "I was afraid we were going to have to keep her on the sixth-floor landing forever. But here she is—right where she belongs. Isn't it wonderful?"

"It certainly is." Buck watched the horse hungrily gobbling up the last of the breakfast food. "And the most wonderful part of all you haven't even mentioned."

"What's that?"

"I can finally go back to eating flapjacks and sausage in the morning."

eleven

When she awoke the next morning, Melinda lay for a moment, trying to remember whether it was really true that she had a horse on the roof or whether she had only dreamed it. Then she leaped out of bed, quickly put on a denim shirt and some blue jeans and was heading for the door when her mother called her back. Reluctantly, Melinda took time to eat breakfast. Then she hurried out the door and up the stairs to the roof.

The sun was shining brightly. A few drops of dew still sparkled on the grass. The white paint of the board fences gleamed. The air smelled different than city air. It smelled like something familiar. It took her a minute to remember what. It smelled like the air of Baffles Falls.

Marshmallow was standing in the middle of the pasture. She raised her head and looked at Melinda, then resumed eating. The girl lifted her arms over her head, stretching them. She climbed between the second and third boards of the fence and started walking slowly toward the horse .But then her pace quickened and by the time she was halfway across the rooftop field she was running. She threw her arms around the mare's neck and hugged her.

Uncle Buck stepped briskly out of the trapdoor to the roof and walked over to the fence. He leaned on the top rail and looked at Melinda, smiling to himself. He started to say something to her, then thought better of it. He walked quietly back to the stairs leading down to the twelfth floor. On the way down them, he met Marcia. He took her arm.

"Let's give the girl another minute or two by herself," he whispered. "She's going to remember this morning a good, long time."

But then Mary Ruth O'Malley arrived and behind her all the other shareholders except Karen Hofstetter, whose mother had insisted she do the breakfast dishes before she went to look at the horse. The girls went rushing up to the roof before Buck could stop them and in a moment Marshmallow was surrounded. Rusty O'Malley came up the stairs, nodding to Buck.

"You really pulled it off, you and the girls," he said. "I wouldn't have believed it. I brought you something that might come in handy."

"A saddle. Now that's mighty thoughful of you, Mr. O'Malley."

"Don't forget, my daughter owns twelve dollars and eighteen cents' worth of Marshmallow. When a fellow has a girl who's part owner of a horse, the least he can do is rummage around in the attic and see what he can find. I found this—it's twenty years old, but the leather's held up pretty well."

The two men watched the girls and Marshmallow. Some of the horse's owners were brushing her, some were combing her mane, several were just standing back and admiring her.

"One thing this horse won't lack is attention," O'Malley said. He raised his voice. "Any of you girls interested in trying out this saddle?"

The response was enthusiastic. Buck saddled up Marshmallow. He took off her halter and substituted a bit and reins. Then he stood back.

"Any of you girls know anything about riding?" They shook their heads. "Then I guess I ought to try her out first."

"I'm sure I can ride her all right, Uncle Buck," Melinda said. "She likes me."

"Sure she does, girl. But you can never tell about a horse. Not many of them will hurt you deliberately, but they don't always behave the way they should. Let me just take her around the pasture a few times to make sure how she handles."

Buck swung nimbly into the saddle. He clucked to the horse, who moved off with a regretful glance at the grass she'd been eating. He put her into a trot, then a canter. The girls watched anxiously. He pulled back on the reins. Marshmallow stopped at once and stood waiting for the next command. Buck leaned over and patted her neck. Then he turned her head around and she walked back to where the others were standing.

"Somebody's done a good job of training her," Buck said, stepping down from the saddle. "She does exactly what you tell her. Now the only problem is that you girls have got to learn how to tell her the right things in the right way so she don't get confused."

He told them about always getting into the saddle from the left side, how to hold the reins, how to use their knees to help control the horse. Then he stepped aside and asked who would be first. Melinda looked around at the other girls. They were all looking at her.

"How are we going to decide?" she asked.

"It's already decided," Marcia said. "Marshmallow's partly ours, but he's mostly yours. We'll get our chance when you come back."

Melinda had never been on a horse before. For a moment she wondered if she really wanted to be there. Marshmallow's back seemed so high from the ground. Then she reached over and rubbed her hand against the arched neck.

"Get up," she said.

The horse moved off obediently and Melinda's doubts vanished. She felt just the way she'd always known she would feel if she ever had a horse of her own to ride.

All the girls got a turn before the morning was over. Several of them put the horse into a trot, but none was quite ready to gallop yet. Buck kept a watchful eye on them, but Marshmallow seemed to sense that she was carrying inexperienced riders and treated them accordingly.

After a while, Buck was satisfied that it was safe. He walked over and stretched out in the hammock, keeping one eye open to watch the girls. Harvey arrived, bringing several small boys and some rocks with him, and began to construct a frog pond in one corner of the pasture. Mrs. Denton came to the roof and went to work planting petunias around the outside of the white board fence near the edge of the roof. Toward evening Sylvester arrived home from work and began to tinker with the catapult he was building to shoot a fishing line from the roof to the river.

Mrs. Denton and the other mothers brought sandwiches to the roof and the families picnicked at the edge of the pasture. It was dusk by the time the other girls began to head reluctantly back to their apartments. Finally, no one was left except Melinda and her great-uncle. Buck seemed to be sleeping, but when she came toward the hammock he opened one eye.

"You can take another ride on my horse if you want to," Melinda told him. "Of course, she's a little tired."

"I bet she is. You look a little weary yourself, girl."

"I can hardly move. But I feel wonderful. This has been the best day of my whole life."

Buck grinned. He reached out and rumpled Melinda's hair.

"I've been around a lot longer than a young filly like you," he told her. "And it's been one of the best days I can remember, too."

twelve

As the summer wore on, the minority stockholders spent most of their free time on the rooftop. They rode the horse, groomed her, or just sat in a row like blackbirds on the top rail of the fence and admired her. Before many weeks had passed, all of the girls could ride pretty well, although Melinda was the most expert. But then, as she told herself, she lived closest to the roof so she spent more time there, practicing.

Marshmallow didn't seem to care that the pasture was twelve stories above the street. The grass grew as fast as the mare's strong teeth cut it down. Each evening, as a special treat, Uncle Buck dumped a box of Buckwheat Roasties in the manger. The cereal company had promised him a lifetime supply and it was as good as its word, although several vice-presidents spend an entire morning debating how it was possible for one man to eat so much cereal.

As the girls became better riders, they began to wish they could do something besides canter around the pasture.

"There's a place to go riding in the park," Marcia

told Melinda. "It would be nice to take her down there. I bet she'd like it, too."

"But she'd have to climb down twelve flights of stairs and back up again."

"Let's ask your uncle. He knows a lot about horses."

Buck gave the matter his serious consideration, once they'd awakened him. He sat on the edge of the hammock and looked at the horse.

"As long as she's going to be a city horse," he said, "I guess we ought to show her the sights. I don't suppose she'd want to climb to the top of the Empire State Building or watch the show at Radio City Music Hall, but she'd be interested in visiting the park, all right."

"Do you think we can get her down the stairs and up again?" Melinda asked.

"Sure. I'll just go ahead with the Buckwheat Roasties. You round up the other girls."

When all the shareholders had arrived, Melinda saddled the mare and Uncle Buck sprinkled a trail of breakfast food that led down the stairway. Marshmallow clattered down the stairs, eating as she went. Everything went fine until they got halfway to the ground level. The girls didn't want the horse to linger long on Mrs. Pontey's floor, so Buck didn't put any cereal on the sixth-floor landing. This turned out to be a mistake.

Marshmallow knew her rights. She'd eaten Buckwheat Roasties on the other floors and she didn't intend to leave the sixth until she'd had some there. She began to whinny loudly and paw the floor. Buck had gone ahead to finish laying the trail, carrying the supply of breakfast food with him.

"Shh," Melinda told the horse. "Come ahead, now. There's more on the stairway."

"Hurry," Marcia said, shoving the horse on. "I hear

somebody coming down the hall. Can't you make her go?"

"I'm pulling as hard as I can. The rest of you keep shoving."

But the mare had made up her mind not to leave just yet. She began sniffing in the corners, but she raised her head just as the hallway door opened. For a long moment, Mrs. Pontey and the horse looked at each other. Then Marshmallow snorted and Mrs. Pontey screamed. Her husband come bounding out of their apartment, his face covered with shaving cream. Mrs. Pontey pointed a trembling finger.

"A horse. There's a horse on the stairway."

Mr. Pontey walked over to peer around the doorway. He nodded his head.

"Yes," he said. "So there is. Good morning, girls. That's a nice animal you've got there. A big one, too."

"Is that all you've got to say?" his wife demanded. "Well, you may want to live in an apartment house that's been turned into a stable, but I don't. I'm going to call the landlord. I'm going to tell him to get over here at once."

Uncle Buck walked back upstairs to the landing just as Mrs. Pontey hurried down the hall and into her apartment, slamming the door. He gave Marshmallow a generous handful of Roasties and the horse and the minority stockholders continued down the stairs to the ground floor. But the prospect of a pleasant day in the park was spoiled.

It had been so long since Marshmallow had been in a place where she could gallop far in one direction without falling off a roof that it took her a while to get used to the park. But the girls kept urging her on and soon she began to enjoy her new freedom. Everyone was pleasantly tired, including the horse, when they walked back to Whetstone Manor. Mrs. Pontey was standing in the doorway to the building, her arms folded. Canelli, the owner, was beside her. Uncle Buck was with them, looking worried and angry.

"I told you they had a horse," Mrs. Pontey said, triumphantly. "I told you they'd turned your roof into a barnyard."

"That animal doesn't live here in my apartment house, does she?" Canelli asked, hopefully. "You girls are just going to keep walking right on by, I trust."

"Of course that beast lives here," Mrs. Pontey said. "If you were any kind of landlord, you'd know what was going on without my having to tell you."

"Now see here," Uncle Buck said. "There's nothing in the rules posted in the lobby that says tenants can't have horses. I been looking it over since all this hullabaloo broke out, and there's not a word about raising horses."

"There's nothing there about keeping elephants in the living rooms or raising crocodiles in the bathtubs, either," Canelli said. "It's just that I never figured the question would come up. Your lease giving you possession of my roof doesn't say you can keep a horse up there."

"It doesn't say I can't, either."

"Enough of this conversation," Mrs. Pontey said. "I will not live in an apartment house that allows horses, and that's final. Either the horse goes or I do."

They had all moved into the lobby by this time, including Marshmallow. The landlord looked at the horse, who was eying the potted palm speculatively. Then Canelli looked at Mrs. Pontey.

"It's a choice between you and the horse?"

Mrs. Pontey put her lips together in a grim line. Buck took the landlord's arm.

"I can see where that's a hard choice to make," he said, winking at Canelli. "Although if it was me, I know which one I'd pick. Why don't we go on up to the roof and talk about it?"

The landlord said that would be a good idea, particularly as he wanted to see what was going on up there. He watched in amazement as the girls led Marshmallow up the stairway as Buck walked ahead with the cereal box.

Melinda turned Marshmallow loose in the pasture and then came back to where the two men were standing, with the other girls forming an anxious semicircle around them. The look on Canelli's face was one of pure amazement.

"I never saw anything like it. When that troublemaker down on the sixth floor called me up and claimed there was a pasture up here and a horse to go with it, I thought she'd finally flipped her wig."

"We haven't really hurt your roof any, Mr. Canelli," Melinda said.

"Hurt it, young lady? No, I wouldn't say you've hurt it. You've transformed it, that's what you've done. It's downright beautiful—all this grass and white fences and everything. I even like the looks of the horse. It's a shame I'm going to have to make you get rid of her."

"But we can't get rid of Marshmallow," Melinda said. "We just can't."

"Couldn't you get rid of Mrs. Pontey instead?" Buck suggested. "To my mind, she does a lot less for Whetstone Manor than the horse does."

"I'd like nothing better. I'm a man who likes his tenants to stay off his back. I don't like the ones who call me up and complain. Mrs. Pontey's always pestering me about some fool thing. But she's got a lease, so I can't get rid of her. And they pay their rent regular, which means I

don't really want to get rid of her, I guess, even if she is a nuisance."

"Marshmallow never calls you up to complain," Melinda pointed out. "She's no trouble."

"I'm in business, young lady. My business is collecting rent. This rooftop pasture is nice, all right, and I've got nothing personal against your horse. But you don't pay much rent for all this space and I'm in business."

"I admit you're not overcharging us," Buck said. "But there's more than one way for a fellow to make a profit."

"How do you mean?"

"If a fellow owns an apartment building, let's say, he can make money by collecting rents. And he can make money if the value of his property goes up. The way it looks to me, having the only rooftop pasture in town must make Whetstone Manor a pretty choice piece of property."

"Besides, look at the improvements we've made on your property," Melinda added. "There's the grass and the fences and the barn we made out of the scrap lumber Rusty O'Malley gave us."

Canelli thought about it. There was something in what they said, he admitted. Still—

"Why don't you take a stroll around the homestead and think about it some," Buck suggested. "Or better yet, stretch out in my hammock for a spell. I do some of my best thinking in that hammock."

The landlord hesitated. Then he admitted that he was tired—talking to Mrs. Pontey had wearied him. Once he'd stretched out in the hammock and closed his eyes, things looked different to him. Buck told Melinda later that as soon as he saw Canelli lie back in the hammock, he knew things would be all right.

"You won't make us get rid of Marshmallow?" Melinda asked.

"Not just yet, young lady. Now that I've looked around here and seen how much you've improved the appearance of my roof, I'm on your side. But I'm not promising anything. It all depends on how much heat I get from the other tenants. If they make too much of a fuss, the horse will have to go."

Buck shook the landlord's hand. He told him they all appreciated what he was doing and they'd do their best not to cause trouble.

"It's close to suppertime," Buck added. "We'd be glad to have you eat a bite, if you've got the time."

"My wife'll be waiting dinner, so I'd better say no. I'm going to have to leave." He leaned back in the hammock and closed his eyes. "The truth is, I kind of hate to go. I've been living in this neighborhood most of my life, but this is the first time I ever realized how peaceful it could be, lying around, smelling the fresh country air."

Things went on as usual for the next few days, with the girls grooming and riding Marshmallow. But Mrs. Pontey had not given up. Marcia told Melinda what was going on.

"She came to our door with a petition to get rid of the horse. My mother wouldn't sign, of course, but Mrs. Pontey's going around to every apartment, trying to get signatures."

"I didn't know she was that mean," Melinda said. "Why does she act that way? Marshmallow hasn't done anything to her."

"My mother says it's because she doesn't have any kids and she's forgotten what it's like to be a girl and have a horse of your own. My mother says she's got too much time on her hands."

"I wonder how many names she's getting on her petition. If she gets many, Mr. Canelli will have to make us take Marshmallow away. I wish we could follow her around, spying."

"Let's," Marcia said.

But Uncle Buck said it wouldn't be ladylike to sneak around, following Mrs. Pontey.

"Besides, girls aren't much good at that sort of thing. They get to talking or giggling. On the other hand, if you were a small boy—"

Harvey said he'd do the job, providing someone would exercise his frogs. Melinda spent the entire morning herding the frogs back and forth across the pasture while Harvey lurked in hallways or ducked around corners. Toward noon, he came back and made his report.

"She was plenty mad. She didn't get a single signature except her own. Even Mr. Pontey wouldn't sign."

"That's wonderful," Melinda told him. "What did people say when she asked them?"

"Oh, different things. The places where there were kids, the mothers mostly got to talking about how much their children had always wanted a horse. Especially when the kids were girls. The mothers'd say, 'My daughter is just crazy about horses.' It made Mrs. Pontey pretty mad. She'd say, 'But I want you to sign this petition to get rid of that beast on the roof,' and the mothers'd say, 'Oh, my daughter's just crazy about horses.' Then Mrs. Pontey would say, 'We mustn't let them turn this apartment house into a stable,' and the mothers'd say, 'Yes, my daughter has always loved horses.' I thought it was a [illegible]tty silly conversation. I guess Mrs. Pontey did, too. [illegible] face would turn red and she'd go away."

[illegible]t some of the tenants don't have children. What [illegible]hem?"

"It depended on who came to the door. If it was the husband he'd take one look at Mrs. Pontey and say, 'Just a minute, I'll get my wife.' If the wife came to the door and heard what the petition was about, she'd say something about how Mrs. Pontey was probably right and they'd talk for a while. But before long, the lady would get a funny look on her face and she'd say, 'You know, Mrs. Pontey, when I was a girl I always wanted a horse.' And then she wouldn't sign, either."

"Do you suppose every woman wanted a horse when she was a girl?" Marcia asked. "Poor Mrs. Pontey. I almost feel sorry for her."

"Well, I don't," Harvey said. "I got plently tired of following her around and listening to those dumb conversations. I was glad when she finally gave up and went back to her own apartment. Mr. Pontey opened the door and I heard her say, 'Well, at least you'll sign my petition,' and he said no."

"I like Mr. Pontey," Melinda said.

"He said she could make a fool of herself trying to stir up trouble if she wanted to, but leave him out of it. And she said she was going to go down to City Hall."

"City Hall!"

"Yeah. She said she bet it was a violation of the zoning laws to harbor a horse on a roof in this congested neighborhood. She slammed the door right after she said that, so I didn't hear what Mr. Pontey said."

Melinda ran over to Marshmallow and put her arms around the mare's placid neck.

"Don't you worry. If you're against the zoning laws, then I am, too. And if you have to leave, I'll leave, too."

"It could be worse," Harvey said. "Mrs. Pontey could be after my frogs instead of your horse. That'd really be serious."

thirteen

A representative from the building inspector's office was the first to show up in answer to Mrs. Pontey's complaint. He was a short, fat man dressed in a blue suit that was a size too small. He poked his head out of the trapdoor and looked around, blinking in amazement. Then he walked briskly over to where Sylvester Denton was working on his catapult and began talking about how it was against the regulations to harbor a horse.

But Sylvester wasn't interested in discussing horses just then. He started explaining how the catapult would make it possible to shoot a line across the highway and the park into the river and catch fish without leaving the roof. The inspector got interested in spite of himself. It turned out that he liked to fish almost as well as Melinda's father and after a while he decided the roof wasn't a horse pasture at all.

"I can see it's mainly a fishing spot," he told Sylvester. "And as long as it's a fishing spot, it certainly can't be against the zoning laws."

"We do have a horse up here."

"I see you do. But as long as the horse is merely incidental to a wildlife refuge for fishermen, it's hardly worth noting in my report. Why don't you call me when you get that catapult working? I'll come over and help you haul in the fish."

Melinda arrived as the inspector was leaving. She'd hardly had time to find out from her father what had happened when a tall, thin woman climbed up the stairway to the roof. She said she was president of the Woman's Neighborhood Improvement League and she was investigating a complaint from Mrs. Pontey that the rooftop pasture was a blighting influence.

"Only it doesn't look like a blighting influence," she told Melinda. "Those petunias next to the white board fence are lovely. I have some growing in my windowbox but they're positively scrawny. Did you plant those flowers, young lady?"

"No, but my mother did," Melinda told her and hurried downstairs to get Mrs. Denton.

Before long, the two women were discussing petunias and snapdragons and hollyhocks and when the league president left she said she'd decided to suggest to all the members that they get busy and beautify the roofs of their apartment houses.

Melinda told Uncle Buck about the two visitors and how well everything had worked out.

"I guess we don't have to worry about Mrs. Pontey any more," she said, patting Marshmallow's neck.

"Now I wouldn't be too sure about that, girl. When an old biddy like that gets her dander up, you can be sure she won't quit making trouble. People like that don't give up easy."

"Even if she is being so mean about my horse, I feel kind of sorry for her, Uncle Buck."

"Me, too, when you come right down to it. But that

doesn't mean I trust her as far as I could throw that barn over there. She's probably down there on the sixth floor right now, calling up somebody who'll make more trouble for us."

Melinda thought he was wrong. But it turned out that, as usual, Buck knew what he was talking about. Along about dinner time, there was another visitor to the roof. This one was wearing a blue uniform.

When Patrolman Casimir Walsh came stalking out toward where they were standing, Melinda took one look at his stern face and knew that no talk of petunias or fishing catapults would do any good this time.

Buck walked over to meet the policeman. "Hello there, young fellow. Come up for a visit, I see. Well, you're welcome to look around. We aren't concealing any burglars or bank robbers, so far as I know."

"You are Sylvester C. Denton?" Walsh asked, pulling out a notebook.

"Nope. I'm Buck Denton. This here is Melinda."

"And that," the patrolman said, pointing to Marshmallow, "is a horse."

"Can't dispute that, young fellow. Marshmallow is a horse, all right. I don't like to brag, but she's probably the finest animal of her kind in this entire neighborhood."

"The only one, too, I imagine." Walsh allowed himself a brief smile, then became stern again. "Now I hope I won't have any trouble with you, but that horse has got to be evicted from these premises. There's a city ordinance against unnecessary noise in a residential neighborhood."

"Marshmallow doesn't make any unnecessary noise," Melinda said. "If she makes any noise, it's necessary—like whinnying once in a while when she's hungry."

"According to the ordinance, which it is my duty to enforce, no unnecessary noise is permitted. Now I admit the horse isn't doing anything right now but standing there eating grass. But according to the complaint we've received from a citizen of this building, the neighborhood's peace and quiet is being threatened."

"Balderdash," Uncle Buck said. "I know where that complaint come from, and I'm surprised a smart young fellow like you would believe it. Isn't it still true that everybody's innocent until and unless they're proved guilty?"

"Certainly, but—"

"And does the law say anything about that rule not applying to a horse?"

"I guess not, but I've got this complaint here and—"

"Then I'll tell you what you do, young fellow. You come on back up here tonight. You pick the time—I want to be fair about it. You come on up here to the roof and listen as long as you have a mind to. And if Marshmallow's guilty of being a nuisance in the neighborhood, I'll be the first to say she's got to move out."

Patrolman Walsh stood, rocking back and forth from one foot to the other, thinking about it. Finally, he nodded. He would be back, he said. Buck and Melinda watched him march across the grass to the trapdoor and disappear down the stairway.

The policeman returned about ten o'clock that night. Melinda had gone to bed—Buck and her mother had insisted that she couldn't stay on the roof all night, although she'd wanted to. Her great-uncle had assured her he'd stretch out in his hammock and be ready for the official investigation of Mrs. Pontey's latest complaint. Walsh came tiptoeing out on the roof. He was surprised to see Buck. He greeted him without much enthusiasm, but Buck pretended not to notice.

"Now I'll tell you what we'll do, young fellow. I'll just make myself comfortable down here on the grass and you stretch out in my hammock. You'd be surprised at how much better things look when you're stretched out in a hammock, with the breeze rocking you back and forth."

"I'll stand, if you don't mind," the patrolman said. "Where's the horse?"

"I'm not sure. She's so quiet, it's hard to tell. Oh, yes. There she is, over in the corner of the pasture. She's probably sleeping."

"It looks to me like she's eating grass. I can see her plain enough with this bright moon. She's certainly a big one. I would think she'd make a lot of noise, tramping around on the roof."

"Not when the roof's covered with half a foot of pasture land, young fellow. It's a fine, bright night, isn't it? It makes a man glad he's got a place like this to go to enjoy it."

Walsh looked around him. The stars were out. The air smelled sweet. It was late summer and some of the fall flowers were beginning to bloom. The asters had started to open. The chrysanthemums that Mrs. Denton had planted near Harvey's frog pond were in bud.

"I guess I will sit down, at that," the policeman said. "It's been a long day. You've fixed this place up, all right. I never saw anything quite like it."

The two men sat on the grass, leaning their backs against the board fence, and listened to the night sounds. The roar of auto traffic from the expressway near the river was somewhat muted there on the roof, but it was loud enough to be heard. A window slammed in an adjoining apartment house. Down on the street, someone laughed loudly.

"It doesn't sound much like the country, does it?" Walsh said.

"You've got to shut the city sounds out. After a while, you get so you can just set here, lean back and imagine you're not in New York at all."

"And what's the matter with New York? I was born and raised here."

"Not a thing's wrong with it, young fellow. It's a great place in a lot of ways. But you got to admit it's not the country. Listen to the crickets and katydids singing from across the pasture."

"So you've got insects on this roof, have you? I better put that down in my report."

"Not insects. Insects is bugs, like cockroaches and such. Those are crickets and katydids. Don't you like to hear them?"

"Now that you mention it, they do sound sort of friendly. I remember one time when I went camping up in the Finger Lake country and we— But never mind that. I'm up here to investigate a complaint."

"And you're doing a bang-up job of it, too. You sure you're comfortable? The hammock might be better."

"I'm enjoying sitting on the grass. You don't get much chance to sit down in my job, especially on grass. Mostly, I have to tell people not to walk on it."

"Grass likes to be walked on. At least, country grass does. I can't speak for city grass, not having had much experience with it. You hear anything noisy about Marshmallow?"

"The horse? No, to be fair about it. I wouldn't know she was there if I couldn't see her in the moonlight."

"Then you'll have to admit that the old biddy down on the sixth floor hasn't got much of a case, right?"

"I'm just doing my job, Mr. Denton. Matter of fact, I kind of like horses. My daughter's always after me to buy her one. Fat chance. There's no place to keep a horse around here, even if I could afford it on a cop's pay."

"My grand-niece thought that, too. You don't happen to have a nice flat roof in the apartment house where you live, do you? You get a few loads of dirt, spread some grass seed around and—."

"All we've got on my roof is television aerials. Besides, how would it look if I put a horse up there and started breaking the law?"

"There's a law against having pets?"

"There's a law against unnecessary noise. Although, as I was saying, your horse hasn't made a disturbance. Not yet."

They sat for a while, looking at the stars, listening to the night sounds and watching Marshmallow grazing in the moonlit pasture. After a while, Walsh asked if Buck thought it would be all right if he had a smoke, even if he was on duty. Buck said he didn't see why anyone would mind, so the policeman filled his pipe and lit it. When he'd finished smoking, he knocked the ashes out against the fence post and stood up.

The sound aroused Marshmallow's curiosity. She turned her head. She sniffed the air. Then she began to gallop around the pasture.

"She's just showing off a little," Buck said, uneasily. "On a night like this, a horse feels like running."

Walsh said nothing. He leaned against the top board of the fence, watching. Marshmallow began to kick up her heels, snorting. Then she stopped abruptly and lay down on the grass and rolled. When she finished, she climbed to her feet and trotted over toward them, whinnying loudly.

"S-s-h," Buck said, nervously. "Mustn't disturb the neighbors."

The horse sniffed at the policeman's uniform. He drew back. Then he put out his hand and patted her flank.

"She isn't as quiet as you made out, is she?" he said.

"She makes horse noises now and then," Buck admitted. "Of course, all them folks tarryhooting around in their automobiles and slamming windows and walking along the sidewalk, talking and laughing, are making people noises. Maybe they disturb the horse, just like you say she disturbs Mrs. Pontey."

The patrolman laughed. He climbed through the fence and walked back toward the trapdoor.

"You win, old-timer. I won't say it in my report, but it's my unofficial opinion that I'd rather have Marshmallow for my neighbor than I would some of the people I know. Of course, you understand I'm only a cop. I do what I'm told. But if it's up to me, I'm not going to do anything to change the way you've got things arranged up here. I think you've got something that's worth keeping just the way it is."

"Come on back any time you're in the neighborhood," Buck told him, slapping his broad back. "And that girl of yours—tell her she can come and meet Marshmallow, if she has a mind to."

Buck told Melinda the next morning that the policeman had turned out to be a pretty good sort and their troubles with Mrs. Pontey were over, but he was wrong. She kept writing letters and making telephone calls and, in general, pestering everyone she could find at city hall and the police station and finally, about a week after his first visit, Patrolman Walsh was back.

"I'm sorry," he told Melinda. He looked sorry, too, and not nearly as stern as he had seemed the first time. "Like I told your uncle, I didn't find anything wrong up here. But the sergeant says I've got to serve this eviction notice on your horse. Between you and me, the sergeant got his orders from the captain and the captain got his straight from the chief, who's getting mighty tired of listening to some woman who keeps calling up to complain all the time."

Melinda took the paper Walsh held out to her. It was full of words like wherefore and whereas and it looked forbiddingly legal. She tried to read it, but all she saw was the sentence that said they must dispose of Marshmallow within twenty-four hours.

She tried not to, but she began to cry. The patrolman put a fatherly hand on her shoulder. Uncle Buck came hurrying over to see what was going on. She handed him the notice.

"Foolishness and balderdash!" Buck shouted. "Why can't that old biddy mind her own affairs?"

"There are people like her in a lot of neighborhoods," Walsh said, sympathetically. "Now I'll tell you what I'd do if I were you. I'd find some nice place in the country and take your horse out there for a few months until the heat's off. By then, maybe Mrs. Pontey will have something else on her mind. Maybe she'll move. Lots of things can happen in a few months. As long as we don't get complaints, we aren't going to bother you. But when a citizen insists, there's nothing the department can do."

"But where can we find a place in the country?" Melinda asked. She rubbed her eyes with the back of her hand. "What if we can't find a good place to take Marshmallow?"

"This order says you've got to dispose of her," Walsh said, unhappily. "If you can't find another place for her—"

"We'll find one," Uncle Buck said. "It doesn't look like this piece of paper gives us much choice."

fourteen

Maybe Carstairs was not a man who reached a decision easily. Ordinarily he saw both sides of everything and spent a lot of time debating which one to choose. But when Uncle Buck telephoned him and told him Marshmallow would have to be disposed of within twenty-four hours, he hung up the phone and jumped in his truck and arrived in front of Whetstone Manor without a moment's delay.

"Load that mare in the back here," he told Melinda. "Maybe she'll eat me out of house and home and maybe she won't, but I'm not going to let some city ordinance do harm to a horse I once owned. She can have a home with me as long as she needs it. And no maybes about it."

They watched the truck drive off down the street with Marshmallow standing in the back of it, placidly eating the hay Carstairs had brought with him. Uncle Buck and Melinda turned and looked at each other.

"It might be all for the best, girl," he told her. "She'll have lots of open space. When the colt's born, she'll be able to let it run."

"But I won't be there to help take care of it."

"That mare will make out all right, don't you worry. And we'll go up and see her every chance we get. Your dad won't mind driving us, particularly if he can take his fishing rod along."

They still had their pasture. The grass was turning brown now, for it was late October and the nights were cold. Melinda and her great-uncle went up to the roof sometimes. But it looked so lonely without the horse that they soon went downstairs again. Buck claimed that he didn't care much for his hammock because lying in a hammock was something you did in the summer, but Melinda noticed that he didn't use it even when the sun was warm.

Sylvester was sympathetic. He spent a lot of his spare time driving Melinda to the country, pretending that he was interested in going only so he could catch some fish. They always seemed to wind up at the fishing holes on Maybe Carstairs' place, however. The horse was glad to see her. Uncle Buck took a week's supply of Buckwheat Roasties with him on such trips and fed them to Marshmallow, who stood in her stall munching her favorite breakfast food while Melinda combed her mane.

"You think she looks happy, Uncle Buck?" Melinda asked after one of the trips to the country.

"She's fat and healthy-looking. Carstairs is taking good care of her."

"But she's always standing there with her head hanging down when we come, as if she was thinking about something."

"Horses don't spend much time worrying about things as a general rule."

"And then sometimes she lifts her head and looks around, as though she's listening for something."

"It's a good place for a horse, out there in the country," Buck insisted.

But he took a careful look at Marshmallow on the next

visit. He tried not to let Melinda see that he was examining the mare, but she wasn't fooled.

"Is she all right, Uncle Buck?"

"Sure she is. Only she doesn't seem to have much pep."

"Maybe it's because she's going to have a colt next spring."

"That could have something to do with it, maybe. I'm no horse doctor, but I know something about such things and I can't find a thing wrong with her that I can put my finger on. But she doesn't act quite right."

As the winter wore on, it seemed to Melinda that Marshmallow looked at her reproachfully each time she had to leave after one of her visits to the Carstairs place. Buck said the horse's listlessness might be due to the cold weather and having to spend most of the time in the barn to keep out of the snow. But he didn't say it as though he entirely believed it.

It was a Sunday afternoon in March when they decided to call the veterinarian. Buck had brought an armload of Buckwheat Roasties, as usual. He opened the boxes and poured the cereal into the horse's manger. Marshmallow only looked at it and sighed. Buck stared at her in disbelief. Then he started for the house on a dead run.

Melinda got into the kitchen in time to hear Buck say something into the telephone about the vet coming right away.

"Of course I'm sure it's an emergency, Doc," he added. "When a horse won't eat Buckwheat Roasties, there's got to be something wrong."

That led to quite a long discussion with the veterinarian, but Buck finally hung up.

"I don't know what they teach them young fellows in horse-doctor school nowadays," he told Melinda. "Doc Arnold didn't even know that Buckwheat Roasties was a horse food. He'd know if he ever tried to eat it himself, I can tell you."

Dr. Arnold gave Marshmallow a thorough examination as Melinda and Buck watched him anxiously. Finally he stood back and stared at the horse for several minutes without saying anything. Melinda kept quiet as long as she could, but she couldn't wait forever.

"She's going to be all right, isn't she, Doctor? She's just got to be."

"There's nothing physically wrong with her, as far as I can tell," the vet said. "Still, I don't like the way she looks. There's something about her attitude that isn't right."

"How you mean, Doc?" Buck asked.

"A mare that'll soon have a colt usually stands around peacefully eating hay and waiting. But this one seems all nervous and upset. I can remember only one other case like this. It was a horse that'd been used to roaming around a large, open pasture. It was sold to a riding academy in the city. It couldn't get used to being a city horse. But that hardly applies to Marshmallow. She's living in the country, with plenty of space and fresh air."

"Could it work both ways?" Melinda asked. "If a horse was used to living in the city, could she get homesick if you took her to the country?"

"Certainly. Horses are creatures of habit. A horse that got used to city noises and smells might have trouble adjusting to life in the country. Has Marshmallow been raised in the city?"

"Not exactly raised there," Buck told him. "But she did seem mighty happy there in her pasture twelve stories up in the air."

The veterinarian stared at him.

"I must have misunderstood you. It sounded like you said the pasture was twelve stories up."

"There isn't a thing wrong with your ears, Doc. The pasture happens to be on a roof. The mare was doing fine there until an old biddy raised so much Ned that we had to bring her here to Maybe's farm."

"That's a shame, Mr. Denton. It's plain to see that Marshmallow thinks of that rooftop as home and wants to go back there. There isn't any way you can take her back, I suppose?"

"What will happen if we don't?" Melinda asked.

" I can't say for sure. But I've seen horses who were disturbed about something who wouldn't eat. And it sometimes happens that a mare that isn't contented doesn't take proper care of her colt. Perhaps you can find some other twelve-story building with a pasture on its roof and put Marshmallow there, at least until after the colt is born."

"There isn't any other pasture like our pasture," Buck said.

"Then we'll just have to hope for the best."

After the veterinarian had gone, Buck and Melinda consulted with Maybe Carstairs on what they should do.

"I guess maybe I could sit around the barn, banging stove lids together and yelling and slamming windows and making other city noises," Carstairs said. "On the other hand, maybe that wouldn't fool her at all."

"I don't think it would," Melinda said.

"Maybe we could fix up a place for her on the roof of my barn. It's kind of slanty, but maybe she's used to being up high and would like it better."

"There's just no way of making Marshmallow believe she's on her home pasture," Buck said. "Except one, and that's to take her back up there where she belongs."

"But what about Mrs. Pontey?" Melinda asked. "If she complains, they'll make us get rid of her again."

"We've just got to be smarter and sneakier than she is, that's all. Somehow or other, we've got to keep that old biddy from knowing there's a horse on the roof."

They decided Marshmallow should be brought back to Whetstone Manor late at night, when Mrs. Pontey would be sound asleep. Carstairs agreed to haul the mare in his truck. They waited until nearly midnight before they set out for the city. Two hours later, when they pulled up in front of the apartment house, Melinda was relieved to see that no lights were showing on the sixth floor.

"I just thought of another problem," she told her uncle. "How can we make Marshmallow walk up all those stairs? She doesn't like Buckwheat Roasties any more."

But when Marshmallow walked down the planks from the truck, she sniffed the air and walked into the lobby without being told. She made straight for the stairway, then looked at Uncle Buck expectantly. He placed a trail of breakfast food ahead of her as she climbed the stairs to the twelfth floor.

"It wasn't that she didn't like the stuff," he told Melinda, "just being homesick ruined her appetite."

When they led the horse through the trapdoor, she trotted around the pasture, sniffing at the fence and stopping now and then to hold her head up and listen to the familiar city sounds. Then Marshmallow kicked up her heels, whinnied, and threw herself down to roll luxuriously in the new spring grass. Melinda ran over and gave her a hug.

"You're home, girl," she said. "And nobody's going to make you go away again."

"We hope," Buck added, under his breath.

fifteen

Trying to conceal a horse is not easy. The other girls who owned shares in Marshmallow met with Melinda and made plans. It was decided that the only way to keep Mrs. Pontey from finding out was to keep her away from the roof.

"We'll take turns standing guard on the sixth floor," Melinda said. "As soon as she punches the 'up' button for the elevator, the guard will run up the stairs and tell the rest of us."

"That won't be fast enough," Marcia Shapiro said. "My brother has a walkie-talkie set we can borrow. Whoever's on guard can call for help on that."

"But what'll we do if Mrs. Pontey does start toward the roof?" Karen Hofstetter asked. "We can't just tackle her and hold her down or she'll get suspicious."

"We'll make a list of things we can do," Melinda said. "Who'll take the first turn at guard duty?"

"I will," Nancy Gormley said. "I always wanted to be a private eye."

Mrs. Pontey came out of her apartment only once that morning, and then she went downstairs and not up. Karen was on guard at the time. She took the next elevator and got to the lobby in time to see Mrs. Pontey walking down the street. She reported to the roof on the walkie-talkie.

"Keep watching," Melinda ordered. "When she comes back, make sure she gets off at the sixth floor."

"Suppose she does come up here," Marcia said. "Should we hide Marshmallow in the barn?"

"She's sure to look there. We've got to think of something better than that. If we had something big enough to cover a horse it might help."

"How about an old blanket?"

"It wouldn't be large enough. Maybe we could sew two blankets together."

"I think Mrs. Pontey might get suspicious if she saw Marshmallow out in the middle of the pasture covered with blankets," Nancy Gormley said.

"I've got an idea," Melinda said. "Everybody get as many old blankets as you can find and meet me here."

When the girls got back, she had strung a clothesline across one corner of the pasture. It was just high enough so that when they fastened one end of the blankets to the rope, the other edge touched the ground. The girls agreed that if they could get Marshmallow to stay behind this row of blankets, no one would be able to see her.

"I hope we don't have to try it, though," Marcia said. "All Mrs. Pontey would have to do is walk over and look around the edge. And she's just nosey enough to do it."

After a few days, it occurred to Mrs. Pontey that every time she went outside her apartment there was a girl hanging around in the hallway.

"They're up to something," she told her husband.

"So what's the harm? Let them stand in the hall—they aren't bothering anybody."

"I think they're watching me. It's mighty suspicious. They're always carrying a walkie-talkie. Well, they can't pull the wool over my eyes, I can tell you that. I'm going to see what's going on."

Mrs. Pontey stalked out of her apartment, glared at Melinda, who was on guard duty, and punched the "up" button. Melinda ducked around the corner and spoke into her walkie-talkie.

"Red alert, red alert. Use plan B."

"Roger," Marcia answered from the roof. "Over and out."

Plan B called for locking the trapdoor and putting three one-hundred-pound bags of oats on top of it. When Mrs. Pontey got there and found she couldn't get out on the roof, her suspicions were confirmed. She marched down to the Denton apartment and banged on the door. Mrs. Denton answered it.

"Your daughter is up to something," Mrs .Pontey said. "I'm a tenant in this building and I have a right to go out on that roof if I want to. And I do want to. I'm coming back up here in a half hour and you had better tell Melinda to have the door unlocked or I'll call the police and break it down."

Melinda arrived just in time to hear the threat. She ducked back around the corner of the stairway until Mrs. Pontey had gone back downstairs, then went into the apartment. Mrs. Denton told her Mrs. Pontey was within her rights in demanding entrance to the roof.

"But what will we do?" Melinda asked. "We can't let her see Marshmallow."

"I'll turn my frogs loose on her," Harvey suggested.

"She won't be afraid of a frog."

"Not one, maybe. But I've got lots of them. Come on."

Melinda used the walkie-talkie to tell Marcia to unlock the door. Harvey went with her to the roof. He gathered up a bushel basket full of frogs. He turned the basket bottom side up, with its edge resting on the edge of the trapdoor.

When Mrs. Pontey came back, she pounded on the trapdoor. There was no answer. Cautiously, she pushed against it. The door was unlocked this time and it opened easily. With a smile of triumph, Mrs. Pontey shoved it hard. The bushel basket did a backflip through the air. Startled frogs erupted from it like popcorn from a popper.

"Help!" Mrs. Pontey flailed about with her arms. "Help, police! It's raining frogs!"

She went galloping back down the stairs, taking them three at a time. Most of the frogs quit chasing her before she reached the sixth floor, but one indignant bullfrog pursued her right up to her apartment door. When she slammed it in his face, he sat in the hallway grunting angrily until Harvey sneaked downstairs and retrieved him.

"That ought to teach her not to stick her nose where it doesn't belong," Marcia said. "I'll bet she doesn't come back."

But Mrs. Pontey didn't give up that easily. After she'd regained her breath, she felt foolish about running away from something as harmless as a basketful of frogs. The more she thought about it, the angrier she got. Finally, she armed herself with a broom and marched back up the stairway.

This time when she opened the trapdoor, Harvey's frogs were not on guard. He had decided they deserved a reward for their efforts and had them over on the far corner of the roof, feeding them bits of raw hamburger. Melinda caught a glimpse of Mrs. Pontey's head emerging from the trapdoor. She had just time enough to give Marshmallow a shove behind the row of blankets on the clothesline. Marcia ran over to intercept the visitor.

"How do you do, Mrs. Pontey?" she said, giving her a sickly smile. "Nice weather, isn't it?"

"What are you girls up to, anyway?" Mrs. Pontey demanded, looking around suspiciously. "Do you have that horse back up here?"

Marcia didn't want to lie about it, exactly. On the other hand, she could hardly answer, "yes" to a question like that.

"I don't see any horses, do you, Mrs. Pontey? A horse is quite a big animal. I guess if there was a horse standing out there in the middle of the pasture, you'd be able to see it."

Mrs. Pontey sniffed. She walked over to the stable and threw open the door. She seemed surprised when she saw it was empty. Melinda joined Marcia. They stood nervously watching Mrs. Pontey.

"I always knew she was an old witch," Marcia whispered. "See, she's got her broom."

Melinda had to giggle at that. Mrs. Pontey glared at her.

"You girls think you're pretty smart, don't you. Well, if that horse is up here, I'll find her."

She reached in her pocketbook and pulled out an apple. She walked over to the fence, holding out the apple.

"Here, horsey," she called. "Come get the nice apple, horsey."

Melinda knew that, aside from Buckwheat Roasties, there was nothing Marshmallow like better than an apple.

"I think we ought to go downstairs," she suggested. "You're not wearing a coat, Mrs. Pontey. You might catch cold."

Mrs. Pontey ignored her. She started walking along the outside of the fence near the stable, holding out the apple and calling. The trick worked. The mare caught sight of the apple by peering between two of the blankets on the line. She gave a happy whinny and started straight for Mrs. Pontey. The blankets were in the way. When the horse tried to go between them, two of them came loose from the rope and draped themselves around Marshmallow's shoulders so that they covered her completely. Mrs. Pontey gave a little gasp and drew back when she saw what appeared to be a pile of blankets running toward her. But then one of the blankets fell off. Marshmallow gave a toss of her head and the other dropped to the ground. Mrs. Pontey turned to the girls in triumph.

"I suppose you're going to tell me that isn't a horse."

Melinda shook her head.

"It's a horse, all right. It's the finest horse in the world. And if you'll just let us keep her up here I'll never ask for anything else again as long as I live."

"I certainly will not, young lady. You had your warning. You were told that it's against the rules to have that animal on this roof. I'm going right downstairs and make a telephone call. And when I come back, I'll have a policeman with me."

Mrs. Pontey left just as Marshmallow arrived at the fence. Marcia looked after the woman angrily.

"The least she could've done was leave the apple," she said.

"What'll we do?" Melinda asked. "We can't let them send our horse back to the country again. She'll get homesick and maybe die."

But they could think of no way to prevent it. When they told Uncle Buck about it, he could suggest nothing, either. Still, he did his best to comfort Melinda.

"Maybe something'll happen, girl. Maybe the policeman will tell her to go fly a kite."

"You don't really believe he will, do you, Uncle Buck?"

"No, I guess I don't. I suppose there's nothing to do but call Maybe Carstairs and make plans to take her back to his farm. Don't you worry about it, girl. A lot of horses manage to live in the country. Marshmallow's just going to have to get used to not being a city horse, that's all."

They went down to the Denton apartment and Buck placed a call to Carstairs. There was no answer. He tried several more times that afternoon with the same result. When Sylvester arrived home from work, he overheard Buck trying to make the long-distance call and told him it was no use.

"Maybe isn't home, Buck. He won't be home for several weeks."

"Not home? But we need him. Where is he?"

"Gone fishing up in Canada some place. He's been talking about doing it for months, but he kept wondering if maybe he might just waste his time and not catch anything. Then he finally made up his mind to go. There's no way to reach him up there—he's out in the wilderness somewhere."

"But if we can't keep Marshmallow here and we can't take her to the country, what'll we do?" Melinda asked. "If they tell us we've got to dispose of Marshmallow right away—"

"She'll wind up at the dog pound, I guess," Harvey said. "But don't worry about it, Melinda. We'll still have my frogs."

It took her a long time to go to sleep that night and when she did she dreamed that the horse was being chased around and around the roof by a woman riding on a broomstick. She woke before the sun was up. She lay there for a while, feeling miserable. Finally, she got up and dressed. She went quietly out of the apartment. Uncle Buck hadn't been sleeping well, either. He heard her go. He leaped out of bed and put on his clothes and followed her up to the roof. In the dim light, he couldn't see her, although he was sure she was there.

"Probably come up here to say good-bye," Buck muttered to himself. "I wish I could do something about that old biddy down on the sixth floor. But I guess anything I'd do would be against the law."

He walked over to the stable and opened the door quietly. Melinda was standing next to the stall. He started to speak to her. Then he saw the expression on her face. It was so full of happiness and wonder that he stopped and gazed at her, holding his breath.

After a moment, she turned slowly and caught a glimpse of him. She put her finger to her lips. She motioned to him, pointing into the stall. He tiptoed over.

"Oh, Uncle Buck," he said. "Isn't he beautiful? Isn't he the most beautiful colt you've ever seen?"

sixteen

The colt was mostly legs. As Melinda and Buck watched, he nuzzled his mother's flank, then went tottering off on his first brave exploration of the world. As far as he could tell, the world consisted of the stall. He moved shakily around it, his large brown eyes blinking, eager to take it all in.

Buck gave Melinda's shoulders a squeeze.

"That's as fine a palomino colt as I've ever seen, girl. You like him?"

"He's what I've always wanted. Look at how silky his mane and tail are. Did you ever see such long legs? What's he trying to do?"

"He's getting tired and he's trying to figure out how to lie down. Only the floor's so far away, he can't decide how to go about it. Look out there, boy. Take it easy."

The colt was swaying back and forth. He looked back over his shoulder at Marshmallow, but the mare only regarded him with motherly pride. He took one more step. Then one leg buckled under him and he fell to the straw. Melinda started inside to help him, but Buck told her not to bother.

"That's what he wanted all along, to lay down and rest

a spell. He'll be all right. Colts are pretty well able to take care of themselves, right from the first. When horses ran wild, the colts had to be able to keep up with the herd soon after they were born. Otherwise, a wolf or something might get 'em."

"At least he doesn't have to worry about that," Melinda said. She heard the trapdoor open. "Oh, no! Look who's here. I'd almost rather it was a wolf."

Buck waggled his beard fiercely and marched outside the stable to confront Mrs. Pontey. Patrolman Walsh was with her. He stood, shifting his weight from one foot to the other, looking stern but sympathetic.

"Sorry, Mr. Denton," he said. "But this citizen here has filed another complaint. You know how it is. I've got to do my duty."

"That horse has to go," Mrs. Pontey said. She folded her arms and looked at Melinda and Buck, her expression triumphant. "And if it isn't out of here within one hour, it will have to be destroyed."

"But you can't do that, especially now," Melinda said. "You can't take Marshmallow away from her colt. No one would be that mean. Not even you."

"A colt?" Mrs. Pontey's expression seemed to relax a little. But then her lips hardened into a grim line. "Two horses are even worse than one. Patrolman, do what you're supposed to do."

"I'm sorry," Walsh said. "There are times when I don't especially like my job, and this is one of them. If it was up to me, you could raise all the horses you wanted to up here. But I have my orders."

"Isn't there any way we could at least wait a few weeks?" Melinda asked. "The colt will be bigger and stronger then."

"In a couple of weeks, Maybe Carstairs will be back

from Canada and we can move them up to his place in the country," Buck said. "A couple of weeks wouldn't hurt, would it?"

"What do you say, Mrs. Pontey?" Walsh asked. "That seems fair enough to me."

"I'll agree to no such thing. An apartment-house roof is no place for horses. It's humiliating to live in a building that's been turned into a stable. What will my friends think?"

"What friends is that?" Buck asked, waggling his beard. "The way you act, I doubt if you have any friends."

"That'll be enough of that kind of talk, Mr. Denton. I'm quite within my rights." She turned to Walsh. "Are you going to do what us taxpayers are paying you to do? Or should I call up the chief of police and complain again?"

The policeman looked at Melinda and Buck. He put out his hands helplessly.

"I've got to do it, folks," he said. "All this talk is just making it harder. You've just got to get rid of that horse, one way or another."

"Those horses, you mean," Mrs. Pontey said. "There's two of them now."

Melinda turned away. She looked out across the pasture. The grass was getting green again. There were a few spring dandelions blooming along the fence. Buck put his hand on her arm, but she pulled it away.

"Can I just go inside and be with Marshmallow for a few minutes by myself?" she asked.

"You certainly cannot," Mrs. Pontey said. "It's all a lot of foolishness and I don't have time to—"

But Patrolman Walsh was holding up his hand and frowning down at her.

"Your time isn't all that valuable, lady. You and me

will just stand here quietly for a few minutes and let the girl say good-bye to her horse."

Melinda walked into the stable. She opened the stall door and walked over to Marshmallow. The colt scrambled awkwardly to his feet, alarmed at seeing her, and she allowed herself to reach out and touch his velvety nose for just a moment. Then she threw her arms around the mare's strong neck and buried her face in Marshmallow's mane.

The colt looked at her wonderingly. When she didn't move, he lost interest. He began to explore the stall again, moving one leg shakily after the other. He was stronger than he had been a few minutes before and more adventurous. He tottered around the enclosure until he came to the door, which Melinda had neglected to close. Her back was turned. She didn't see him move on his stiltlike legs out through the opening toward the daylight.

The colt stood blinking in the sun for a moment. Then he headed straight for where the policeman and Mrs. Pontey were standing. Before he had quite reached them, he noticed the grass underfoot. He tried to put his head down to investigate this new phenomenon, but his legs were too long for the rest of him. He lost his balance and staggered over to the fence.

Mrs. Pontey put out her hand to fend him off. The colt looked up at her curiously. He put his nose against her fingers. She pulled back her hand. Then, as though she couldn't quite help herself, she put it back again and rubbed his head.

"Why, he's only a baby," she said.

Uncle Buck snorted.

"Most things is, when they've only been born a few minutes ago."

"But he's so soft. And why does he walk so funny?"

"He walks a lot better'n you could at his age," Buck told her, waggling his white beard.

Mrs. Pontey glared at him. But when she turned back to the colt, her expression softened. Buck started to say something more, but then he thought better of it. He caught Walsh's eye and winked at him.

"Colts is mighty appealing creatures," he said. "Of course, they aren't really worth much at that age. They can't do anything useful. I suppose the best thing to do is haul them off to the dog pound."

The men glanced at Mrs. Pontey, but she paid no attention to them. She put out her hand again and the colt licked her fingers.

"You know what I always wanted when I was a little girl?" she said, talking mostly to herself. "I'd forgotten, but it comes back now. I used to lie awake in my room and think about it. Of course, we lived in the city and there was no place for one. But I always wanted a colt of my own."

Melinda came hurrying out of the stable, looking for the colt. She stopped when she saw Mrs. Pontey standing next to him, rubbing the animal's neck.

"What's happening, Uncle Buck?" she said. "What's going on?"

"Oh, nothing so surprising. Mrs. Pontey's just made a very interesting discovery, that's all. She was just saying that she used to be a girl once herself."

"Well, I haven't got all day to stand around here," Patrolman Walsh said, briskly. "I'm bound to enforce the law. As long as there's been a complaint, I've got no choice but to serve notice that you've got to get your horse off this roof at once. When we drew up the papers we didn't know you had two animals up here, so I'll have to go back to the station house and get the document changed. But it won't take me long to get back."

"Don't you dare," Mrs. Pontey said.

"But, lady—You're the one who filed the complaint."

"Never you mind about that. This colt likes me. Look at how he's standing here, letting me pat him. You touch a hair on his head and I'll complain all the way up to the mayor."

Walsh grinned at Uncle Buck, who grinned back. Melinda looked at Mrs. Pontey in wonder.

"Then I don't have to get rid of Marshmallow?"

Mrs. Pontey frowned.

"I still don't think much of having a full-grown horse on the roof," she said. "Still, I suppose my young friend here needs his mother. But if I withdraw my complaint, you've got to promise me one thing."

"I'll promise. Whatever it is, I'll promise."

"When I come up here to see your colt, and maybe bring him an apple or some carrots, you tell your brother to keep his frogs locked up."

Later in the day, when Melinda told him, Harvey said that was okay with him.

"Even if Mrs. Pontey does like colts," he said, "my frogs'd just as soon not have anything more to do with her. She ran down those stairs so fast when they chased her that she made them all jumpy."